Praise for *Dead to Rights*

Dead to Rights is a relentless, high-octane thriller that hits hard and doesn't let up. Case Younger—former Army Ranger and Air Marshal—is a man haunted by guilt but driven by justice. With enemies closing in and the past weighing heavy, he fights like a man with nothing to lose. Gary Quesenberry delivers explosive action, razor-sharp twists, and a hero who bleeds battles and never backs down. If you love your thrillers packed with grit, heart, and edge-of-your-seat action, this one's for you!
—Alan C. Mack, U.S. Army CW5 Retired, author of
 Razor 03, A Night Stalker's Wars

Case Younger keeps getting better! *Homecoming* was a thrill ride with a heart of gold, and *Dead to Rights* follows up on the promise made by that debut. Quesenberry takes a dash of Jack Ryan's focus, a pinch of Spenser's moral compass, and a dram of Jack Reacher's precisely applied violence. Quesenberry mixes it all together with his own real-deal experience and cooks up an adventure story that leaves you wanting more! Do not miss out on this new member of the righteous mayhem A-team.
—Jason Brick, author of *Safest Family on the Block*,
 There I Was…When Nothing Happened, and
 The Bushido Chronicles

Gary Quesenberry's *Dead to Rights* is a hard-hitting follow-up to *Homecoming* and one you don't want to miss. A domestic-based thriller, it kicks off like a flash-bang through the breach and doesn't relent until the last page. This is a gripping tale with characters that feel real and a hero we genuinely need. Quesenberry's blend of diving action and value-based emotion will resonate with the readers of Taylor Moore's *Garret Kohl* series or Ryan Steck's *Matthew Redd* saga. Gripping and immersive, I can't wait for the next installment in this series

—Delbert A. Roll, MAJ (Ret), United States Army, CIA Operations Officer (Retired), owner of Greencastle Associates Consulting, author of *Lessons in Professional Relationship Management from a CIA Operations Officer*

It's gritty, satisfying, and most importantly, enthralling! As soon as I finished reading *Dead To Rights*, I wanted to get my hands on the next book in the series. Gary Quesenberry can place the reader in the action and drama that unfolds with meticulous attention to detail on every page. Each character is developed so vividly that you feel like you know them and will find yourself loving the heroes and hating the villains. This is a completely immersive reading experience, and it became difficult to put the book down as the intensity increased. *Dead To Rights* will quench your thirst for justice but will leave you starving for the next chapter.

—Phil Morden, former Navy SEAL and owner of Element Epic Entertainment

They say you can never really go home again, but that's exactly what Case Younger does in *Dead to Rights*–Quesenberry's riveting follow up to the first Case Younger novel *Homecoming*. Picking up essentially where the first novel left off, this thrilling, layered and edge-of-your-seat second effort in the series sets the tone right out of the gate. What follows for the reader is a complex, smart, and relentless journey filled with fully fleshed out characters that not only build on the successful arc of the first novel in the series, but creates them in a way that feels fully believable, and lived in. It's like you know these people and you viscerally go with them on their journey, feeling all the pain, fear, and struggle that they do along the way. You believe the villains and you relate to Case Younger and the people of the town that are plunged into this adventure. This is an epic and dangerous story filled with action and numerous surprising twists and turns that sweep you into the moment but never feels forced or inauthentic. This time around, Quesenberry has upped the stakes for Younger, who just wants to be left alone as he returns to his hometown friends and family, but unfortunately for him, that is not to be. Ranging from intense action to organic slow burn builds, *Dead to Rights* is a story that keeps you turning the pages. This is an excellent, hard to put down read and an incredibly worthy follow up to Case Younger's first adventure in *Homecoming*. I enjoyed this very much and personally can't wait to see where the Case Younger series takes us next.

—Jude Gerard Prest, showrunner, director, writer, CEO for LifeLike Productions, Inc., numerous award-winning screenplays including *Harry's File*, *The Los Angeles Diaries* (adaptation), and *Rabbit Hash: Center of the Universe* (feature documentary)

Quesenberry once again drew me into the perilous and suspenseful life of former Federal Air Marshal Case Younger. If you like fast-paced action thrillers that showcase down-to-earth heroes, relatable villains, and second chances, this is your next read.

—Liz Lazarus, author of three thrillers, *Free of Malice, Plea for Justice,* and *Shades of Silence*

DEAD TO RIGHTS

Nonfiction books by Gary Quesenberry:

Spotting Danger Before It Spots You
Spotting Danger Before It Spots Your Kids
Spotting Danger Before It Spots Your Teens
Spotting Danger for Travelers

Fiction by Gary Quesenberry:

Homecoming
(Book one in the Case Younger series)

DEAD TO RIGHTS

A CASE YOUNGER THRILLER

GARY QUESENBERRY

YMAA Publication Center
Wolfeboro, NH USA

YMAA Publication Center, Inc.
PO Box 480
Wolfeboro, NH 03894
1-800-669-8892 • www.ymaa.com • info@ymaa.com

ISBN 9781594393655 (print)
ISBN 9781594393679 (hardcover)
ISBN 9781594393662 (ebook)

© 2025 by Gary Quesenberry
All rights reserved including the right of reproduction in whole or in part in any form. Any use of this intellectual property for text and data mining or computational analysis including as training material for artificial intelligence systems is strictly prohibited without express written consent. For permission requests, contact the Publisher.

Edited by: Leslie Takao
Cover Design: Axie Breen

20250530

Publisher's Cataloging in Publication

Names: Quesenberry, Gary, author.
Title: Dead to rights : a Case Younger thriller / Gary Quesenberry.
Description: Wolfeboro, NH USA : YMAA Publication Center, [2025]
Identifiers: LCCN: 2025933896 | ISBN: 9781594393655 (print) | 9781594393679 (hardcover) | 9781594393662 (ebook)
Subjects: LCSH: Home--United States--Fiction. | Peace of mind--Fiction. | Friendship--Fiction. | Retribution--Fiction. | Motorcycle gangs--United States--Fiction. | Justice--Fiction. | Family secrets--Fiction. | Suspense fiction. | LCGFT: Thrillers (Fiction) | Detective and mystery fiction. | BISAC: FICTION / Thrillers / Crime. | FICTION / Mystery & Detective / Hard-Boiled. | FICTION / Small Town & Rural.
Classification: LCC: PS3617.U48 D43 2025 | DDC: 813/.6--dc23

This is a work of fiction. Names, characters, places, and incidents either are the product of the author's imagination or are used fictitiously, and any resemblance to actual persons, living or dead, businesses, companies, events, or locales is entirely coincidental.

Printed in USA.

For the warfighters.

"The most terrifying force of death comes from the hands of men who wanted to be left alone. They try, so very hard to mind their own business and provide for themselves and those they love. They resist every impulse to fight back, knowing the forced and permanent change of life that will come from it. They know that the moment they fight back, their lives, as they have lived them, are over. The moment the men who wanted to be left alone are forced to fight back, it is a form of suicide. They are literally killing off who they used to be, which is why, when forced to take up violence, these men who wanted to be left alone fight with unholy vengeance against those who murdered their former lives. They fight with raw hate and a drive that cannot be fathomed by those who are merely playacting at politics and terror. True terror will arrive at these people's door, and they will cry, scream, and beg for mercy, but it will fall upon the deaf ears of the men who just wanted to be left alone."

—Author Unknown

PROLOGUE

Reggie Stansfield knew his time was up. Word spread rapidly through the neighborhood that the police had been spotted—and not just any police, but police with big, black SUVs more in line with a SWAT team than a patrol cop. They'd first shown up three days ago, circling the block at random hours and parking on the street across from the Regency Heights housing complex. They didn't interact with anyone, chase away the vagrants or make arrests. They simply watched.

Standing at the window of his fourth-floor apartment, Reggie looked up and down the trash-strewn alleyway. He didn't see the dealers, bums, or hookers that typically inhabited the streets around this part of Baltimore—a telltale sign that something was about to go down. He didn't know who they were or what they'd be coming for, but Reggie wasn't taking any chances.

"Leo, we gotta go." He yelled from the bedroom as he shoved the last of his necessities into a big brown canvas bag—toothbrush, computer, a portable laser printer that didn't incorporate the microscopic forensic watermarking found in off-the-shelf brands, his various stamps and seals, and a stack of ten blank Belgian passports he'd purchased off the black market. Everything else he'd packed up days ago when the SUVs first showed up.

"I'm gettin' there. How much time do we have?"

"Everybody's ghosted. They have to be close. Just grab what you can, and let's get the hell out of here."

Reggie frantically searched the plastic folding table he used as his workspace for the flash drive he'd been given. Without it, he was fucked. He repeatedly glanced at the Hi-Point model C-9 pistol lying on the nightstand by the bed. This was stressing him out. He hated guns. He was just the documents guy, but Leo had insisted that he always keep one on him, just in case. It looked like that "just in case" moment had finally arrived.

The flash drive was essential to Reggie's business. It contained the names, photos, and personal information he needed to finish the passports—ten girls, ten passports, a forty-thousand-dollar payday. It was a no-brainer. He knew what was happening, these girls were being trafficked, but he never had to see or interact them, which made his job a little bit easier. Sometimes, he'd lay awake at night, seeing their faces—little girls, some no older than twelve, condemned to a life of sex and servitude. It was a lot to deal with, but the money made up for what little sleep he'd lost. Once completed, the passports were handed over to Leo, who walked them down the street and stashed them in locker J94 at the Greyhound bus station. Whatever happened to them after that was above Reggie's pay grade. Unfortunately for Reggie the stolen blanks cost eight grand apiece, and the money he'd used to purchase them wasn't his. Financing came from men at the top, with much deeper pockets and way more to lose if they got caught. Reggie didn't want to find out what happened if he failed them.

Gotcha. Reggie saw the portable drive lying on the carpet beneath the makeshift desk. Somehow, the tiny device had been knocked off in his rush to leave. Just as he bent to pick it up, he heard tires screeching in the alleyway. He looked out the window again to see three men with ARs dressed in body armor rolling out of one of the black SUVs and storming through the side entrance.

"Fuck! Times up, Leo. They're coming!"

Reggie stood still and listened. Plenty of wanted men lived between the ground floor of Regency Heights and Reggie's apartment. Hopefully, it was one of them the police were after. The seconds rolled past in his mind, each a tiny reminder of the bad decisions that led him to this moment—*ten…nine…eight.* He should have heard something by now. Shouts of protest from furious wives, babies crying, gunshots, something. But it was quiet. The only sound Reggie heard was Leo racking his pistol from the living room.

Three…two…one…Fuck!

The blast rocked Reggie back on his feet. The only thing he could hear now was an intense ringing in his ears and the faint, pop, pop, pop of weapons fire coming from the other room. It was over. Reggie stumbled toward the nightstand and grabbed the pistol Leo had given him—one he barely knew how to use. It was heavier than he remembered, but he gripped it the way Leo had taught him and waited. He knew he'd never make it in prison. The people he worked for had men on the inside, rough men who would never again know life on the streets. He doubted he'd last a week. Even if he could get away, there was nowhere to hide. The people involved in this operation were well connected and had eyes on everyone and everything. This was it—his last stand.

As the ringing in his ears subsided, Reggie heard someone shouting. "Clear," from the other room, then it was quiet again. He stood there, his palms sweating as he tightened his grip on the pistol and raised it toward the door. How did he ever get himself into this mess? He'd had a decent job working for Customs and Border Protection, good benefits, and a steady work schedule, but the allure of fast money and the promise of a lavish lifestyle had pulled him away from all that. Now, here he was, standing with his back against the wall of a filthy apartment, prepared to die for rich men he'd never even met.

As the door crashed inward, Reggie panicked and pulled the trigger. At first, he thought the weapon had misfired. The stress he was experiencing had started systematically shutting down the bodily functions that were secondary to his survival—like hearing. The man in front of him fell to the ground, but that was the last thing his mind could register. As quickly as the first man had entered the room, a second was right behind him, weapon up. There were bright flashes of light and the brief sensation of falling, then nothing. Reggie was dead before his body hit the floor.

Part One

Impact

Chapter 1

For the most part, outlaw bikers have a reputation for being dirty—dirty clothes, dirty bikes, and dirty deeds. It was a cultivated image that separated them from the rest of polite society and kept unwanted attention away from their business. Most found it easier to operate within the sordid ecosystem of drugs, distributors, pimps, and prostitutes when they looked the part. But JC Wilks, the Sergeant at Arms for Richmond's chapter of the Dead Rebels, was different. JC was clean-cut, handsome, and well-educated, which allowed him certain freedoms unavailable to the rest of his kind. When he was on his bike and wearing the denim cut that identified him as a fully patched member of the club, the level of brutality he brought to the job earned him fear and respect. But for every ounce of violence that lurked beneath his Ivy League exterior, there was an equal measure of cunning and charm. JC could easily change into one of his Brioni suits and be as comfortable sitting around a boardroom table as he was in the leather seat of his custom Harley Deluxe. This duality is what made JC so valuable to the Dead Rebels, and it's the reason he'd been sent, on their behalf, to negotiate a new trafficking route between Virginia and New York. But now he was back in Richmond, and things were not going well.

Born Jonathan Cornelius Wilks, JC had been raised in a very affluent suburb of Baltimore by his mother, Madison, who stayed alone in their stately Victorian home while his Father commuted into the city where he worked as a defense attorney.

His dad, Jonathan Senior, was often distant and preoccupied when he was around, and his mother was usually into her fourth glass of wine by noon. That left JC to explore his own path in life, which, through various proclivities and turns of events, had landed him here— identifying the charred remains of his friends.

JC turned to the detective standing by the door of the cold, white-tiled room. "So, explain to me again how my friends ended up burning alive in their own bar."

Detective Donaldson was a veteran cop who'd been in the Dead Rebels' pocket since he was a rookie. He knew JC well enough to be afraid of him and cautious with his answers.

"All we know right now is that this was a calculated hit. Whoever it was knew the club's routine and where they'd be the evening of the fire. It looks like he hit the Decatur house first after these guys rolled out." Donaldson said, motioning toward the bodies, "Then, waited at the Spoke for the officers meeting. There was no sign of forced entry at the house, and I seriously doubt anyone let him in, so he either had the key or the skills to pick the lock. Either way, it all looks professional. Very efficient. He must have been watching your crew for a while."

"Anyone besides the girls there at the time?"

"One of your prospects. But the girls all vouched for his innocence, said he was a perfect little angel and did nothing wrong, so we cut him loose and haven't seen him since."

"You keep saying 'he.' How do you know one man did all of this?"

"Your prospect was able to tell us there was only one man inside the house. The guy choked him out and tied him up but otherwise didn't hurt him."

"Did you get a description?"

"A man a little over six-foot tall, athletic, black jacket, black ballcap, blue eyes. That's about it."

JC's eyes scanned the steel tables that displayed the burnt remains of five Dead Rebels. He chuckled quietly at the irony. "Any video footage?"

"None. The bar had cameras, but they were all inside—no outside surveillance. There was, however, an ATM across from the parking lot, but the angle was off. The only thing it caught was one of your girls staggering up the street just past the Spoke."

"Did anyone pick her up?"

"Yeah. We have her down at county. She doesn't know anything, but we figured you'd want to talk to her before we cut her loose."

JC nodded and walked slowly around the room, placing his hand gently on the blackened flesh of each Dead Rebel. Donaldson grimaced at the morbidity of it all and looked away. JC turned abruptly toward the door.

"Go get the car."

Priscilla Reynolds, "Prissy," as she was known to the club, found herself in the small, dank holding cell, waiting for someone to tell her what she'd done wrong. She'd woken up in a daze, unsure of the time or how long she'd been there. There were no windows or a clock, so it was impossible to tell. She sat up on the narrow steel bed that was bolted to the floor and looked around. A solitary steel toilet sat in the corner, flanked by a small sink with a tiny shatterproof mirror above it. The dirty, off-white walls were scrawled with the names of past occupants, accompanied by colorful descriptions of the cops who'd locked them away. The last few nights were a little fuzzy, but she remembered leaving the house with Tucker for the Rusty Spoke. It wasn't until he went inside that the serious looking man in the old pickup truck told her to leave, and she'd wandered off. Suddenly, there was a fire, then lights and sirens. After that she was scooped up by that damned dirty cop and dropped here—but for what?

That's when she heard the keys.

"Prissy."

It was the cop.

"You got somebody here to see you."

Could it be Tucker? She liked Tucker. He was a bit heavy-handed, but he always took her for rides on the bike and let her wait outside the Spoke while he drank with the boys. Maybe he could fill her in on what was happening.

"Tucker, is that you?"

"No, Prissy, it's not Tucker."

Oh shit! She recognized the voice. It was JC, the good-looking one from up north. JC was different. He didn't have any tattoos or a criminal record that she knew of. Most guys in the club liked to brag about that kind of thing, but JC never did. He was intelligent and charming, and my God, that smile. Prissy was convinced JC's smile could melt the paint off a Cadillac, but she knew he had a reputation for violence, and that always scared her, so she did her best to stay away from him.

"Where's Tucker?" She asked.

JC rounded the corner, absent the charming smile. Instead, his face was stern and unsettling.

"Open the door, Donaldson."

Prissy backed away instinctively as Detective Donaldson searched for the key.

"Look, I didn't do anything wrong," she said. "I just did what Tucker told me to, I swear."

Donaldson inserted the big, brass Folger Adam key into the lock and twisted, making a loud echoey *clank*. JC entered the cell and stopped just shy of Prissy, who now cowered against the back wall.

"I'm sorry, JC. I didn't do anything wrong, really."

JC put a hand on her shoulder. His touch felt warm and tender until he squeezed. "I know, Prissy. I'm not upset with you, but I have some bad news."

Prissy looked up wearily and waited for JC to continue.

"Tucker's dead, Prissy. They all are, and I'm going to need your help to figure out who did it. Okay?"

Prissy was shocked and a little saddened. She wasn't like the other girls. She'd come to the club on her own—a runaway teen looking for money and a place to stay. Tucker had taken her in. She didn't cry. Prissy knew that things like this happened when you lived the type of life Tucker had, so she just nodded. JC turned and motioned toward the open cell door.

"I can go?" Prissy asked no one in particular.

"After you help me find the person responsible for this, you're free to go wherever you'd like. Until then, I'll get you out of here and you can come stay with me for a while, okay?"

That made Prissy happy. She'd been locked away in that smelly clubhouse with the other girls for so long that freedom seemed unnatural. The thought of being able to go anywhere she wanted brought a smile to her face. But that smile quickly faded when she looked up into the piercing green eyes of JC Wilks. Freedom, it seemed, would have to wait.

Chapter 2

The door crashed inward as Case Younger hammered just above the deadbolt with a heavy, hand-held battering ram. His teammate Matt covered the opening with his short-barreled HK 416 while Ross tossed a flashbang grenade into the center of the room. The explosion that followed was devastating but completely nonlethal—sending more than one thousand lumens of light and one hundred eighty decibels of sound into the small apartment, enough to temporarily blind and deafen anyone inside. That would allow Case and his team the precious seconds they needed to gain a tactical advantage over the target. Matt immediately stepped inside, sweeping his weapon across the room as he button-hooked left into the far corner. Ross followed closely behind to cover the opposite corner in what looked like a choreographed and deadly dance. As he swung right, he caught movement ahead. A man crouched behind an old sofa in the corner, fumbling with a jammed 1911 pistol. Ross fired three times, following the man down with the red dot on his SBR as he slumped over the couch and dropped the handgun to the floor. Case tossed the battering ram and rushed into the room behind Ross to cover the center. Each man swept their weapons from left to right, covering their sectors of fire. The entire process took only seconds.

"Clear," Matt announced from the left corner, keeping his SBR up and at the ready. Case echoed the word immediately, indicating no further threats within his field of fire.

"I've got one man down in my sector. Moving to secure," Ross yelled from his position by the sofa.

"Move," Case responded as he shifted his field of fire to cover Ross.

Ross rushed to the corner where the man he'd shot lay bleeding. After checking his vitals and confirming that he was indeed dead, Ross zip-tied the man's hands for good measure, cleared the jammed pistol before stowing it in his waistband, then stood and gave one last sweep across the room, "Clear."

Two more rooms needed to be secured. The team knew from the blueprints they'd studied prior to the mission that one led to a small bathroom, the other to the apartment's single bedroom. They entered the bathroom first and came up empty. Case found himself taking point as the team stacked on the final door. He stood to the right and noticed the absence of hinges, meaning the door swung inward. Case took a deep breath, then felt the deliberate squeeze on his shoulder, indicating that the men behind him were ready. Case kicked the door hard, shattering the lock, and rushed inside, where he was immediately met by gunfire.

The first round struck Case in the center of his chest, knocking him back and causing him to fall. Matt continued into his sector then fired at the person attacking from the other side of the room. Blood painted the faded yellow wall behind the culprit as Matt's second round struck him on the bridge of his nose, immediately destroying the central nervous system. The man fell to the floor, dead.

Again, Ross swept the room, announcing "Clear" before moving toward Case to render aid.

"You okay, buddy?" Ross asked, smiling as he looked down at Case.

Case opened his eyes and sat up, "Damn, that hurt." He said to no one in particular as he rubbed at the ceramic chest plate tucked inside his body armor.

"Well, this ain't the movies, cowboy. You're lucky we were here to save ya…again," Ross stated sarcastically.

"Don't be a smartass, Ross." Case grumbled as he got to his feet. "Is that him?"

Matt knelt in the corner, matching what was left of the man's face to the photo they'd taken from the file.

"Yeah. This is him alright."

Case walked across the small, cluttered room and looked down at the lifeless body of Reginald "Reggie" Stansfield, one of the many accomplices to what had transpired in Case's hometown of Pikesville, Virginia.

Six months earlier, after leaving the federal air marshal service and returning home, Case had discovered and dismantled a meth operation being run by the Dead Rebels Motorcycle Club. In doing so, he also uncovered the club's more nefarious plan to kidnap and sell young girls into a sex trafficking ring centered in Baltimore. A man named Rex Kelley, who worked for the club, took it upon himself to feed new girls into the system through force or coercion. After being drugged and beaten into compliance, the girls were then driven into the city where a network of pimps, handlers, document suppliers, and transporters sent them to various parts of the world, never to be heard from again. Rex, in return, was handsomely paid. Case had recused several of the ring's victims before finding files the Dead Rebels had been keeping on each person working within the trafficking chain. Case took those files to his former FAM teammates, Matt Barrett and Ross Davenport, who now worked as contract employees for a joint task force subordinate to the FBI. Their contracts with the CIA had been terminated at the request of a man named Andre Brown and new independent contract agreements signed for a special branch known as the Critical Missions Project. Thankfully, Matt had convinced Case to pursue the remaining members of the trafficking ring legally instead of going after them alone. The last thing anyone wanted to see was for Case to wind up in prison. Now, after jumping through a series of hoops to make Case an official member of the team, they'd systematically killed or apprehended every person affiliated in any way with the trafficking operation. Reggie here was the last.

Case studied the body a little longer. "Damn good work fellas. I can't thank you enough."

"The pleasure was all ours," Matt said as he stood, inspecting the hole in Case's vest. "Wow. That was a close one."

"Yeah. Do me a favor, and don't tell Sam. Okay?"

Matt laughed but could see Case was serious. After returning to Pikesville, Case had reconnected with his former girlfriend, Samantha Raines. Now that this was over, he hoped to return home and settle into a quiet life on the family farm with Sam and her daughter Mia. But she wouldn't want to hear stories about Case getting shot in the chest as a result of everything that had happened.

"Oh, you don't think you're just gonna run off to your little dream life down south and stick me and Matt with all the paperwork, do you?" Ross said from the doorway.

Case smiled. "I wouldn't dream of it, buddy. But the quicker we get this mess tied up, the quicker I can put everything behind me and get back home."

"You still don't want to tell us what happened that brought us here in the first place?" Matt asked.

"Trust me, Matt. The less you know about that, the better."

"Plausible deniability, right?" Ross added as he rummaged through the dead man's pantry. "Anybody want some pretzels? I'm starving."

Matt shook his head. "Fair enough, but we still have work to do. Let's start taking some photos and rounding up phones, computers, thumb drives—anything we can find that may lead to more connections within the trafficking ring. Put those in the Faraday bag so no one can remotely wipe it. Then we'll hand everything off to forensics and wrap this shit up. Sound good?"

With that, the team went to work, careful not to unintentionally alter any electronic data that may lead to more raids or arrests. Once everything was properly documented and stored, the team called in the cleanup crew and returned to the blacked-out van that had driven them to their final target. Case sat on the webbed bench seat and removed his plate carrier, carefully studying the small hole in its center. He took out his Spyderco folding knife and pried a 9mm hollow-point bullet from the vest's thick nylon cover. The impact had caused the round to flatten and mushroom outward, giving it a flower-like appearance. Case rolled the projectile around in the palm of his hand. It reminded him of the tulips his mother used to plant around the house. He knew he'd gotten lucky, and he also knew luck was never a good strategy for survival. It was time to go. Case placed the bullet in the sleeve pocket of his black MultiCam shirt, then rested his head against the cold steel wall of the van. It had been a long night, and as his eyes slowly began to close, all he could think about was home.

Chapter 3

Samantha Raines moved hurriedly around the house as her daughter Mia and Mia's boyfriend Trevor tried to help her find her car keys. She was still settling into life at Case's place, and the stress of not having him around and the feelings that erupted at random after the violent beating she'd received from the Dead Rebels was starting to seep out in unexpected ways. She searched under the bedroom dresser and kitchen table. She looked on every counter and, in every cabinet, but still, nothing. Exasperated, she threw herself into the old recliner in the front room and sighed.

"Mom, are you sure they're not still hanging in your ignition?"

"I'm sure, Mia. I came in from work last night and put them right here on the counter like I always do."

"Were you wearing your coat, ma'am?" Trevor asked from beneath the coffee table as he searched under the couch with the light from his cell phone.

"Umm, I believe so. Why?"

Mia rolled her eyes as Trevor stood and walked over to the coat rack. He stuck his hand into the right-side outer pocket and retrieved a jumbled set of keys attached to a long, blue and gold Cook County High School lanyard. Trevor whistled at the heft and bounced the keys in his hand, smiling. "How in the world do you lose something this big?"

"Give me those, smarty," Sam said as she stood and snatched the keys from Trevor. "Don't you kids need to get to school?"

Sam really liked Trevor. He'd always had a crush on Mia and now, since Case had saved her from Rex and his gang, the boy always seemed to be around. He was loyal and trustworthy, and he reminded Sam a lot of Case when he was that age, just absent the temper. After the Grandview mess was cleaned up, Case invited Sam and Mia to move into his family's farmhouse on the northern edge of Pikesville. It was safe and secluded, plus Trevor and his grandpa Dimpsey lived just a few hundred yards across the road. She felt at home here but still found it hard to relax sometimes. She hadn't heard a word from Case in several weeks, and it was starting to worry her. This is how it all happened before. Case had lost his temper and got into a fight before he left for the army. That landed him in jail. His dad had smoothed things over with the sheriff at the time, but once he was out of Pikesville, the letters became fewer and farther between; the calls eventually stopped, and in the end, he just never came back. Sam snapped out of her malaise when Mia yelled from the hallway.

"Okay, Mom," Mia shouted, "We're leavin'. I love you."

"I love you too. You kids be careful, and no speedin', Trevor!"

Sam fell back into the living room recliner, exasperated, and watched through the rusty screen door as Mia climbed into the big gray Dodge truck Case had given Trevor before he left. Trevor loved that truck, but it only reminded Sam that Case had been uncertain about coming home. He'd caused a lot of damage in Pikesville by taking out the Dead Rebels. Jesse, Mia's biological father who assisted in her kidnapping, was now dead—shot in the chest by his drug dealing partner, Rex. Sheriff Sunny Brewer had committed suicide—disgraced by his involvement in the operation, and Case had left eight more bodies scattered throughout the mountains surrounding

Grandview Trailer Park, where the whole nightmare had taken place. Luckily, Case's brother, Bobby, had taken over as acting sheriff and, with the help of a friend in the State Police, fixed the entire thing to look like a gang dispute. Knowing the fight wasn't over, Case had left town to pursue what remained of the gang and end the ordeal for good. He'd told Sam before driving away that it was the only way to keep her and Mia safe, and she believed him. Case promised he'd come back to her, but it had been six months, and aside from a few brief and cryptic phone calls, Sam had no idea where he was or what he was doing. Just as she started to feel at her lowest, the phone rang, and Case's number appeared on the screen.

"Case?" Sam answered excitedly.

"Hey, Sam."

Sam felt a wave of relief and emotion at the sound of Case's voice.

"Case, are you okay? Where are you?"

"I'm fine, Sam," Case assured her. "I'm up north with Matt and Ross. I just wanted to tell—"

"Case, are you in trouble? Did you do anything else to—"

"Sam," Case interrupted, "I'm okay, and no, I'm not in any trouble."

"Good." Sam sighed into the phone.

Case could hear the relief in her voice and changed the subject. "Bobby told me you got in touch with him and started goin' to the range. Are you okay?"

In truth, Sam had been struggling with the aftermath of what happened, but felt it was important for Case to stay focused on what he was doing. So, she sat up a little straighter and spoke with a confidence she knew would put Case's mind at ease. "Yes, I did. And as it turns out, I'm a pretty good shot.

I've even outshot a few of Bobby's deputies."

"Good. I'm glad to hear that. I never want you to feel—"

Now it was Sam's turn to interrupt. "Case, I'm more prepared now than I've ever been in my life. I've had Bobby take us to the range once a week, and Dimpsey's been teaching me about home defense and surveillance detection. I had a security system installed here at the house. Hell, Amanda even signed me and Crystal up for a women's self-defense course at the rec center. We've all been going together—Mia too."

Case was silent. He knew he was the reason Sam and Mia had been targeted in the first place and he felt horrible about it. "Sam, I—"

Sam stopped him again before he could apologize. "Case, after what happened I made a decision. No one will ever put a hand on me or Mia again without a serious fight on their hands. I won't be caught off guard a second time."

"You're an incredible woman, Sam. I'm proud of you."

"Oh, you just wait till you get home, mister. I have a few Jiu Jitsu moves I can't wait to try out on you."

Case chuckled, "Well, start warming up, champ. Because I'll be home soon."

"You're coming back?" Sam said standing, unable to contain her excitement.

"Yes, Sam. I'm coming home. It's over."

Sam felt tears gathering in her eyes as she fought to maintain her composure. "Okay. You don't know how happy that makes me, Case."

"Me too, Sam. I love you."

Sam couldn't hold it back any longer. Silent tears streamed down her face as she smiled. That was the first time Case had told her he loved her since high school.

"I love you too, Case. Get home soon, okay?"

"I'll be there in three days. We still have some debriefs to attend, but I'm headed back to Pikesville as soon as that's done. I have to go, but I'll see you soon."

With that, Case hung up the phone. Sam wiped her eyes. Looking down at the keys in her hand, she'd forgotten why she needed them in the first place. But none of that mattered now. Case was coming home, and life, she hoped, would finally start to feel normal again.

Chapter 4

Edith Flack had lived in the same house on Decatur Street in Richmond for most of her life. Her father had been a warehouse foreman for a big tire company and bought the small two-story townhome when it was new, and the neighborhood was still somewhat respectable. A lot had changed over the years. The tire plant had closed decades ago, her parents had passed on, and the neighborhood slipped into the steady decline that most middle-class areas suffer from once all the good-paying jobs disappear. She'd paid the house off long ago, but Edith was almost eighty now, eking by on what little she drew from social security and the few dollars her twenty-year-old grandson, Jerry, brought in from his job as a stock boy at the local supermarket. He was a good boy but suffered from a mild form of autism and, at times, was more than Edith could handle. Her only solace came from quiet evenings spent doing her word searches in front of the television while repeats of Wheel of Fortune played in the background. But it seemed now that even her time with Pat Sajak was destined to be interrupted. Someone was at the door, so Edith shuffled toward the entrance in her robe and slippers, uncertain of who could be calling at such an hour.

"Okay, okay, I'm coming. Just give an old woman time. Jerry dear, are you awake?" She yelled up the stairs. "Someone's here."

When Edith opened the door, she didn't expect to see such a handsome, well-dressed man standing on her stoop at 10:00

p.m. The neighborhood was typically inhabited by those noisy bikers, so this was a pleasant surprise. Edith smiled.

"Hello, Ma'am. I'm sorry to bother you so late in the evening. My name is JC Wilks, and I work for a firm of private investigators," JC lied. "It seems that there's been a string of home invasions in this area, and my company has been tasked with tracking down the culprits."

Edith eyed the man skeptically. "Why aren't the police handling that?" She asked.

"Well, ma'am. The police have been busy with more pressing matters, so they contracted my firm to handle some of their less egregious cases." JC said as he smiled his most charming smile.

"Oh, my." Edith said, "Well, I don't know how I could be of any help with that, but I certainly want to see these delinquents arrested. It's those bikers, you know. I'm here most days alone. My grandson Jerry works—"

JC felt his temper flare at the mention of his dead comrades. Not because he gave a shit about any of them, but because it reminded him of the setback this whole ordeal had caused him. "I apologize, ma'am, but I'm in a bit of a hurry. I just noticed that you had a video doorbell and was hoping you could let me review any footage that may have captured a glimpse of our suspects."

"Oh, that confounded thing. My grandson put that in. He said to keep me safe, but I don't see how—"

"Is Jerry home?" The man interrupted again.

"Yes, he is, but he has to work in the morning. So, I don't think—"

"Ma'am, my assignment is of the utmost importance," JC said as he pushed past Mrs. Flack and into the house. "Do you think you could just call Jerry down here for me so we can figure this out? It'll only take a second. I promise."

"Well, okay," The old woman said as she closed the door behind him. "Jerry! Can you come down here, please?" She called up the stairs again, her voice now showing signs of fear. "There's a man here to see you."

Prissy sat in the car across the street from JC and watched as he stepped inside the elderly lady's home. She knew what JC was after. She'd given him the description of the truck she saw at the Rusty Spoke the night of the fire, an old, blueish truck with big tires. She also told him what she could remember of the man she saw on the street that night—the very serious-looking man with blue eyes who told her to walk away. JC had been doing everything he could to find that truck and the man who drove it. Now, after a week of searching, he believed what he was looking for lay on the other side of Mrs. Flack's doorbell.

He'd been inside for a while, and things were quiet, so it scared Prissy when she heard the gunshots. Two quick bangs accompanied by bright flashes of light spilled from the downstairs windows. It made Prissy jump in her seat. JC stepped outside as if nothing had happened. His face lit by the faint glow of a cell phone.

"Okay, you ready to go?" He asked as he slid into the driver's seat.

"Sure," Prissy answered, too scared to ask about the woman inside. "Did you get what you needed?"

"I sure did," JC said as he held the cell phone up in front of Prissy. She noticed the tiny droplets of blood he'd tried to wipe away, leaving light pink streaks across the screen. On it, she saw the image of a blue/gray pickup truck with big tires turning the corner in front of Mrs. Flack's townhome. JC used two fingers to zoom in on the image and smiled as a Virginia license plate filled the tiny screen.

"I got you, you son of a bitch." JC snarled. "Now, let's go have Donaldson find out who our new best friend is. Whadaya say?"

Prissy sat silently in the passenger seat, too afraid to speak. She knew whoever was inside that house was dead, and she had no intention of being next. Her only chance of surviving this was to stay compliant and useful.

Prissy swallowed. Her mouth was dry and felt as if it were about to crack. "Sounds good, JC. Let's go get this asshole."

Chapter 5

Case strode down the long white corridor of the JTF headquarters building just outside McLean, Virginia. Sun from the center courtyard spilled through the narrow windows, casting angular, alternating patterns of light and dark across the freshly waxed floor. He felt a bit out of place wearing his jeans, Silverado work boots, and t-shirt, so he made sure his access badge was prominently displayed, letting everyone know he belonged there regardless of his appearance. He nodded politely at the suited intel analysts carrying stacks of files from one secure conference room to the next. They all looked fresh out of high school to Case—an unfortunate side effect of growing older.

He came to the end of the hallway and knocked on the door of Andre Brown's office. Andre had been working within the Critical Missions Project for nearly three years. He'd transferred over from the Secret Service, where he served honorably on President Carlisle's personal protection detail. When someone made an attempt on her life at the inauguration rally, Brown had pinned the newly elected president behind a concrete pillar and shielded her from sniper fire until she could be evacuated. He was shot twice and lost his left eye in the process but shunned any type of recognition for the act, asking only to be kept in the service of his country. In return for saving her life, President Carlisle created the CMP under the purview of the Federal Bureau of Investigations and put Brown in charge—answerable only to the Director.

"Come in."

Case walked into the sparsely decorated office and stood. A large framed picture of the founding fathers signing the Declaration of Independence was hanging on the far wall. Attached to the frame was a small brass placard that read—*When tyranny becomes law, rebellion becomes duty*—a quote from fellow Virginian, Thomas Jefferson. That was the only personal item Andre had in his office aside from a photo of his daughter, Tracy, sitting on the corner of his deck. He was never one to discuss personal matters freely, but had confided in Case that she'd recently received an athletic scholarship to run track and field for the Naval Academy in Annapolis, Maryland. Andre may not have been talkative, but he was a good man and a proud father.

"You wanted to see me, sir?"

"Have a seat, please." Andre said pointing at the two hard plastic chairs across from his desk.

Case sat and waited.

In the past three years, Andre had assembled an elite team of former soldiers and law enforcement officers capable of deploying anywhere within the United States to quickly and, more importantly, quietly dispose of any threats to the safety and security of the American people. After the hijacking of Flight 759, Matt and Ross left the Federal Air Marshal Service to contract with the CIA, but were quickly acquired by Mr. Brown and made a part of the CMP. They had convinced Andre to bring Case in temporarily to shut down the human trafficking operation being run out of Baltimore. Now that the assignment was over. Case would be debriefed by Andre and sent on his way.

"Case. We appreciate the work you put in." Brown started. "Matt and Ross were right about you."

"Well, sir, I may agree or disagree depending on what they told you. But I'm glad the guys talked me into coming to you with this."

Case felt like he owed everything to Matt and Ross. They had served together in the FAM Service for more than eight years and had covered each other's backs in more inhospitable countries than Case cared to remember. In the aftermath of the Flight 759 hijacking and the loss of his protegee, Rebecca, they'd been the ones who kept him grounded—kept him from losing his mind in front of the press, and been more than willing to help when he came to them with the files he'd discovered on the trafficking ring. They were indeed his chosen brothers.

"They told me you originally planned to take this on alone."

Case considered his response and kept his answer simple. "Yes, I was."

"You know, the more I looked into it, the more I saw that there were some 'convenient' deaths in and around this trafficking organization," Andre said as he folded his large hands on the desk and stared bluntly at Case. The man refused to wear an eye patch to cover his injuries, and it unsettled Case, which was the exact effect Brown was looking for. It kept people honest.

"Sir, I—" Case began before he was cut short.

"But," Brown continued before Case could say more, "these gang disputes can sometimes be confusing and, quite frankly, unsolvable. All I know is this. Between what those two have told me and what I've personally witnessed during the last several months. There will always be a place here for you if you want it."

"I appreciate that, sir, but I have people I need to get back to in Pikesville. I've been away long enough."

"Well," Brown said, standing, his muscular frame casting a

shadow over the desk in front of him. "The offer is always on the table should you change your mind. Otherwise, I wish you the best of luck back home."

With that, the two men shook hands and parted ways. Case walked back down the hall to the cubical he'd been assigned for administrative work. There were twelve cubicles, one for each team member, separated by a narrow pathway leading to a small kitchen area. It wasn't much, but it had a full-size refrigerator, stocked cupboard, and coffee maker next to a carousel of Black Rifle Coffee K-cups. It looked more like a space for rookie analysts, but it seemed even door-kickers weren't immune from the red tape that accompanied governmental action. He grabbed the single personal item he'd brought with him—a picture of Sam and Mia he'd taken before leaving Pikesville. The two stood on the front porch of the home he'd grown up in. Sam's arm was draped over Mia's shoulder and the two smiled brightly. It was a sight Case couldn't wait to get back to.

"You taking off already?" Ross said as he entered the small bullpen.

"I have to get back home, buddy, but I'd love to have you and Matt come down sometime so we can catch up under less stressful circumstances."

Ross chuckled. "You mean to tell me there's a side of you that doesn't like getting shot at?"

"Believe it or not, I just want to go home and be left alone, Ross."

"Well, Matt's out on an Op. He's gonna hate that he missed you, but you know we'll always be there for ya. Whatever you need."

"You've proven that time and time again, my friend. I won't forget this."

Ross frowned sarcastically. "Stop it before we both start cryin' and wantin' to braid each other's hair and shit. This isn't the Army, ya know."

"Asshole." Case said smiling.

"I love you too, buddy. Now get back to that woman of yours before she changes her mind about you." Ross quipped as he walked away, biting into an apple he'd stolen from Matt's mini-fridge. "And no more cowboy shit, okay?" He added over his shoulder before disappearing around the corner.

"Yeah, no more cowboy shit," Case said to himself as he tucked the picture into the pocket of his t-shirt and walked away. It was time to head home and put this whole damned mess behind him for good.

Chapter 6

Detective Donaldson sat at his desk, brushing his skinny fingers across the thin strands of dark brown hair that lay across his head. He was never one to be overly concerned about his appearance. He'd been wearing the same suit for three days, for God's sake, but when Monique from accounting mentioned he was "looking a little thin on top," it bothered him. Now, he did his best to cover it up with what little hair he had left.

He'd been a cop for over fifteen years. He started with the best of intentions. He was bright and diligent but soon realized how little money being a police officer brought in. It only took a year's worth of overtime shifts at local high school basketball games, grocery stores, and construction sites until he started looking for other ways to make ends meet. That's when he responded to a domestic violence call in the McGuire District of Richmond.

When he showed up, the first thing he noticed was a string of Harley Davidsons parked diagonally against the curb, fronts facing the road. He was met on the porch steps by a man in a jean vest. A rectangular patch on the left was embroidered with the word *Richmond* in the center, and another on the right read *President*—a biker. His name was Greg, but everyone in the house just called him *Lucky*. Donaldson had informed the man that he'd received a call indicating that a woman had been assaulted in the front yard. When he asked if he could step inside and take a look, Lucky was all too willing to oblige. The place was a mess and reeked of stale beer and marijuana. Drug paraphernalia was openly displayed on the tables and girls who were obviously underage lie around the house in various stages of undress. It didn't take a genius to figure out what was going on. When he turned to confront Lucky, two other men stood behind him with guns pointed at his head.

"Looks like you have a decision to make, officer," Lucky said.

Donaldson knew his only two options were to comply or die. Never one to be the hero, Donaldson chose compliance.

When he left the house, he was a thousand dollars richer and stood to make a lot more by helping the club out whenever they needed it. He wasn't the only dirty cop in Richmond, and he certainly wouldn't be the last, so he shoved the cash-laden envelope in his pocket and left without making an arrest. Now, after more than a decade, the club still liked to remind him of his options. Comply or die. He always chose the option that kept him alive.

Donaldson opened the License Plate Recognition software on his laptop. With it, he could upload the image he'd received from JC, and the OCR or Optical Character Recognition program would scour various databases for information on that particular vehicle and its owner. It could also tap into a network of traffic cameras and track vehicles moving through the interstate system to a specific location. Donaldson grimaced as he sipped at a paper cup of reheated coffee, clicked on the image, dumped it into the program folder, and waited.

It only took a few seconds. "Bingo." Donaldson picked up the phone and dialed JC's number.

"What do you have for me, Donaldson?" JC asked by way of greeting.

"Avis Bartholomew Younger of Pikesville, Virginia. Born

September 23rd, 1949. Deceased as of May 8th, 2012."

"That doesn't tell me who was driving the truck."

"I'm getting there," Donaldson assured JC. "I did some digging. Avis had two sons. One is Robert Younger, a deputy sheriff in Pikesville. Now acting sheriff."

"Is that our man?" JC asked anxiously.

"I thought it may be, but it turns out that on the night of the Rusty Spoke fire, Robert was recovering at home from a collapsed lung, which he suffered after being shot in the chest. This all happened the same night the Pikesville operations went sideways."

"So." JC was growing impatient.

"So, his older brother, Case Younger, was—"

"Wait." JC interrupted again. "Why do I know that name?"

"Because, Case is some big-shot hero. He was the Federal Air Marshal who stopped that hijacking last year. But one of his partners got killed on that flight. I guess he felt responsible. Anyway, he left the air marshal service after the incident and headed back home to Pikesville." Donaldson took another sip of coffee and continued. "He was also an Army Ranger who did three combat tours in Iraq and Afghanistan. He's an expert in weapons, survival, escape and evasion, unconventional warfare, you name it. I guess he saw plenty of action because he accumulated more medals than I care to list. There's a police report in the system that Detective Dillon Wayne of the Virginia State Police filed. It says Case was at a neighbor's house the night the Pikesville operation got destroyed. It was all written off as a gang dispute, but shortly after that, Case disappeared. I pulled every picture I could find, and he matches Prissy's description of the man she saw outside the bar that night. I'll text you the most current photo we have of him. This is your man, JC."

"Good work, Donaldson. Send me the picture. I'll be in touch if I need anything else." JC said before abruptly hanging up the phone.

Walking over to the large floor-to-ceiling windows of his loft apartment, JC looked out over the James River and poured himself another scotch. Prissy lay sleeping on the sofa beside him. At twenty-five, she was older than the girls he was used to but still young enough to be considered attractive. JC had brought her to his apartment to keep an eye on her. He'd removed and hidden the drugs he found stashed in her purse, taken her out shopping for a respectable wardrobe and got her cleaned up, not for her but to protect his own image and to keep her from being recognized. She was breathing softly now, her blond hair draped over the pillows. Prissy had hit a bit of a rough patch coming off the heroin but was leveling out now, which was good. He needed her sharp for what he was about to do. Now that he had his target, he needed a plan. Case Younger wasn't the kind of man you'd expect to go down easy. Killing him would take some thoughtful consideration. JC sipped his Macallan 25 and looked down at the phone when it chimed in his hand. A text from Donaldson. JC tapped the message and watched as a photo of Case Younger filled the tiny screen. The man's face was lean and unsmiling, he had thick wavey brown hair and the same penetrating blue eyes Prissy had described. He didn't look as if he were police or military, but there was a hardness about him that gave JC pause. If this man was as dangerous as Donaldson suggested, he was going to need some help.

Stonehill Investment Group's headquarters sat on the 52nd floor of One Vanderbilt, situated next to Grand Central Station between Vanderbilt and Madison Ave. Known simply as the SUMMIT, the building's gleaming exterior stretched to a towering one thousand four hundred feet, allowing for panoramic views of the Hudson and East Rivers, the Plaza Hotel, and the entirety of Central Park, tying together both the private and public sectors of commerce in New York City. In the four thousand square foot lobby, massive stone pillars stood on either side of the long reception desk that separated the spacious entryway from the polished bronze hall leading to the elevator bank, train, and subway terminals connecting the structure to the rest of the city. It was considered the crowning jewel of Midtown Manhattan and a prize location for a prestigious investment banking firm like Stonehill.

Tanner Greene sat in his expansive office reviewing Stonehill's latest acquisition. His firm had just acquired another building on the upper west side of Manhattan, and Tanner was pleased with the bottom line. This deal would bring in a remarkable twenty-six million dollars for the company and another six for Tanner himself. These funds would be routed through the British Virgin Islands to sidestep taxes, and Tanner would walk away one step closer to his dream of becoming a billionaire. He'd worked hard to get where he was, and aside from the somewhat unorthodox methods Greene used to amass his fortune, he'd earned the majority of it legally. Some however had been earned through the selling and transporting of one of the earth's most profitable commodities: women. He didn't think of that side of his business as work but more of an enjoyable hobby that generated a considerable amount of capital.

Growing up, Tanner had never been very good with women.

He was short—just under five and a half feet tall and built in a manner most people would consider soft. His lack of physical strength worried his mother, so she coddled him as a child and never allowed him to be outside unsupervised. On the few occasions Tanner snuck out alone, the result was always the same. He'd return home bruised and bullied. But it was never the other boys who picked on him. They seemed to be indifferent to young Tanner. It was the girls who were relentless and mean. Sure, they were nice enough at first, laughing at his jokes and telling him how cute he was. But they'd recoil when he would put a hand on them or go in for a kiss.

"Don't be gross, Tanner."

"But I thought—"

"Jesus—as if." Then they'd run off giggling and pointing with their friends.

It was hurtful and he never forgot it, but no one was laughing at him now. Now, he was in control and could buy, sell, trade, and treat people however he saw fit.

When his phone rang, Tanner looked down and saw it was JC Wilks, the man that had been sent to him from some rustic part of Virginia to set up a new transportation route that would run from the deepest parts of the south up to Richmond, then on to Baltimore. From there, Tanner could take full advantage of the confluence of major highways, casinos, cruise lines, and cargo ports to transport girls around the globe. But that plan was soon thwarted when someone literally burned the entire operation to the ground. Tanner had put JC in charge of finding the people responsible and correcting the issue. If he was successful, Tanner had promised him a position within the firm. A promise he had no intention of keeping.

"You've solved the problem?" Tanner asked.

"Not yet, but I know where to start."

"And where might that be?"

"Pikesville, Virginia. I found the man who did this to us. His name is Case Younger. I'm sure you've heard of him. He's the guy who stopped that hijacking last year."

"Really? Well, that could pose a problem now, couldn't it?"

"Yes, sir. But I have a plan."

"And what will this plan cost me, Mister Wilks?" Greene asked.

"Nothing," JC replied. "I want this man dead just as bad as you do. Not only that, I want everyone he loves to watch him die so they never dream of crossing us again."

Tanner chuckled, "Us, mister Wilks?"

JC ignored the dismissal and continued.

"I can't go at him head-on, Mr. Greene. He's smart, and he's dangerous. If you can send me a few of your security guys, I'll consider that payment enough."

Greene deliberated on the proposition. "Fair enough. I'll send three of my best men to you in Richmond." He paused. "But, Mister Wilks, I expect you to handle this without drawing attention to me or my company. If you compromise Stonehill or me in any way, I will see you buried right beside our friend Case Younger. Do you understand me?"

JC didn't like being threatened. He considered himself too valuable a resource to be treated like an underling. His free hand balled into a fist as he tried to compose himself. "Understood." He answered. "Just send me the men. I'll handle the rest."

The line went dead in Tanner's hand. He looked down over the new spring foliage that was beginning to fill Central Park, ruminating about the mess in Virginia. It reeked of violence, something Tanner abhorred. He didn't particularly care about the consequences of violence. He just didn't like the attention it drew. It made him uneasy and tense, but he'd entertain JC's thirst for advancement as a means to remove an obstacle to profit. Greene walked across to the intercom on his desk and pressed a small red button.

"Yes, mister Greene?" A metallic voice answered from the tiny speaker.

"Celia, I need you to get my head of security in here immediately."

"Yes, sir."

"Oh," Tanner added. "And after you call him, I need you to come see me. I'm feeling a bit tense."

There was a brief pause on the other end, but Celia knew better than to resist. "Yes, Mr. Greene." The girl responded. "I'll be right there."

Chapter 7

Bobby Younger felt overwhelmed, not only because of his new job, but because it seemed that with every day came new and unexpected changes. Since the Grandview incident, Bobby had been appointed acting sheriff pending the next election, and to avoid any conflicts or the appearance of favoritism, his girlfriend, Deputy Amanda Reynolds, had applied for a position as a third-grade teacher at the Pikesville elementary school. She'd always loved kids, and Bobby had never seen her happier than she had been since starting her new job, but he missed having her around the office.

Bobby sat at Amanda's old desk. It was empty now, aside from a few folders and a small glass jar full of pencils and pens. He nudged the jar aside and noticed how much dust had accumulated since she'd been gone. Not wanting to dwell on her absence, he swiveled to face the office door across from where he sat. The word SHERIFF was printed in big block letters across a small square of frosted glass in the center. Bobby hadn't fully committed to taking over Sunny's office yet. The memory of what the man had done was still too fresh in his mind. Part of him wanted to understand how Sunny could have chosen to side with Rex and the Dead Rebels over the people who had treated him like family. But no matter how hard he tried, he couldn't come to grips with what had happened. Sunny had been sick and needed help but was too proud to ask for it from the people closest to him. Instead, he'd turned a blind eye to Rex's business in exchange for the money he needed to cover his cancer treatments. A seemingly innocent gesture, just look the other way and no one gets hurt, but the repercussions of those actions resulted in a lot of people getting hurt, including, Bobby himself.

As he sat there looking across the desolate office, Bobby thought back to Amanda's first callout, a domestic dispute involving two drunken parents and a three-year-old girl named Winnie. When Bobby pulled up, it was late. Red and blue lights reflected harshly off the cracked windows of a rundown trailer. Bags of garbage lined the rickety front porch, and a small bicycle with training wheels lay carelessly in the overgrown yard. The boyfriend in the dispute, a man Bobby had dealt with on a regular basis, was in handcuffs, and the mother was being carted away on public intoxication charges. Bobby walked inside to find Amanda sitting on the floor watching an episode of *Go Dog Go* with Winnie. The little girl's head was in Amanda's lap, and Amanda stroked her hair softly while singing along with the opening theme. Right then, Bobby knew this was the woman he wanted to spend the rest of his life with. That night, at the end of their shift, he got up the nerve to ask her out.

"Ya know, the station could use more of that."

"More of what?" she asked, confused. "Abusive assholes?"

Bobby shook his head, "No, just some compassion. That little girl back there just had a rough night. One of many more to come, I'm sure, but for a while, I believe she felt like she had a friend tonight. Someone she could trust."

Amanda blushed. "I hate seeing children getting treated like they don't matter. They can't help what they're born into. They need an advocate."

Bobby looked at the ground, "Well, you're a good one."

Both walked back to their patrol cars in silence before Bobby spoke again.

"Amanda?"

"Yeah?"

"I'd like to take you to dinner one night if you wouldn't mind."

"It's about time. Aren't we both off tomorrow?" She asked.

Now, it was Bobby's turn to blush. "Pick ya up at six?" He asked with a grin.

Amanda slid into the driver's seat of her car and switched off the light bar. "I'll be looking forward to it."

After years of dating and keeping their relationship a secret, Bobby finally proposed one evening over a romantic dinner for two. He'd bought candles from Dimpsey's Hardware store and, while stuck in the house recovering from his wounds, had even learned to make Chicken Marsala, Amanda's favorite dish. His first three attempts weren't fit to feed stray dogs, but he finally got it right. Happily, she'd said yes, and the wedding date had been set for May 21st. Turning back to the empty desk, Bobby started to have doubts—not about his love for Amanda, but about his ability to be the husband she deserved.

Bobby's mother, Molly, had died when he and Case were young, so their father, Avis, had raised them alone. Avis always did the best he could for his sons, and Bobby loved his dad, but he wanted to be better—not the moody, volatile man his dad had become after losing Molly. Now, after everything that had happened, he wondered if that was possible.

"That's about enough of that." He said as he shook himself from the depressive thoughts and stood to leave. Turning toward the big front windows, Bobby was shocked to see his dad's old Dodge Power Wagon pulling up in the front parking lot. "Case!"

Bobby rushed to the door to greet his brother, and the two

men embraced—a much warmer greeting than when Case initially returned home to Pikesville back in the fall.

"Hey, little brother," Case said as the two men stepped back and looked one another over. "You look good. No more bullet holes since the last time I saw ya?"

Bobby laughed. "I could say the same about you. For some reason, not getting shot seems easier when you're not around. Did you do everything you needed to?" he asked.

"Yes, I did. But it's done now, and I'm home."

"I'm glad to hear that, Case."

"Hey, I wanted to thank you for taking Sam to the range and getting her up to speed."

Bobby brushed the comment aside, "Ah, it was no trouble at all. Hell, she was getting so good she even embarrassed me a few times." Case noticed Bobby fidgeting with the key ring that hung from his belt—a sure sign he had other things on his mind, "But there's something else I feel like you should know, Case. Sam wouldn't want me to mention it, so if you love your little brother, she'd better not find out I said anything."

Case's eyes narrowed, "What's happening Bobby?"

"Sam's struggling. She's putting up a good front. She doesn't want to worry anybody, but you know what the woman's been through—the beating, Mia's kidnapping. I feel like it's all starting to take a toll on her."

Case was more than familiar with the effects of PTSD and the lengths people would go to to keep it hidden. He'd been worried about Sam since he left. "I appreciate you saying something, Bobby. I thought I heard something in her voice when I called the other day, but it's hard to tell over the phone. I won't tell her you said anything. I promise. What about Mia?"

"Hell, she's just like her mama. Tough as a nail, but you can tell it's bothering her too.

Case nodded knowingly but felt like he needed to change the subject, "So, Sam told me the date's been set. Looks like for once my timing is good."

"We still have a few weeks, but I'm glad you'll be here to help out."

"I'm here for whatever you need little brother."

"Good, because I'm not gonna give some big speech or tell ya how honored I'd be, but I don't want to stand up there without you. So, I'm officially asking if you'll be my best man. I just wanted to ask ya in person."

Case smiled, "Are you kidding? I'd be honored. How about you call Amanda and invite her over to the farm after work? Sam's gonna make a big meal, and Dimpsey and Trevor will be coming over. We can all celebrate together, and you can catch me up on what's been happening since I left."

"That sounds perfect."

"Good." Case said as he walked back to the truck. "Now I need to go do some catchin' up of my own. We'll see ya around seven."

After locking up the station, Bobby walked to his car, absentmindedly unsnapping the key ring from his belt and it dawned on him that this had been Case's first stop. After all the doubt and fear building inside him lately about how Case would fit back into his life, that single act helped put Bobby's mind at ease. Case had walked away from Pikesville right out of high school and left Bobby alone to deal with their shell-shocked father. It had left him feeling abandoned by his brother, and they hadn't had much of a chance to reset their relationship since Case had come back home. Now, it felt like things were finally returning to normal—something Bobby had wanted for a very long time.

Chapter 8

Standing at the entrance of Tanner Greene's office, Mike Moretti waited to be let inside. He'd never gotten used to such lavish surroundings. Three tufted leather couches sat around a very expensive-looking coffee table next to the windows overlooking the city. Gold gilded chandeliers hung from the wood-paneled ceiling, and a large, backlit STONEHILL logo dominated the far wall, casting a soft yellowish glow across the black marble slabbed floors. Mr. Greene's assistant, Celia, sat behind a semi-circular desk by the double doors that led into Tanner's office, trying unsuccessfully to hide her tears and a freshly blackened eye.

Celia came to Mr. Greene from UCLA, but not in the manner most college students find an employer. In fact, she'd never even graduated. Back then, she didn't pay much attention to the little changes in her life, but she wished she had. She'd met a boy, Adam—that was the first change. He was a well-read English major, which appealed to Celia, who was an avid reader herself. He was also sweet, charming, and a good listener, so she felt comfortable with him—comfortable enough to eventually tell him about her mom and dad's refusal to help with her tuition. Her parents believed that she needed to pay for everything herself to have a deeper appreciation for her education. So, she worked two jobs to make ends meet and struggled to have the typical social life most college students feely enjoyed.

Adam treated her nicely and helped her out with money from time to time. Initially, she refused, but he was persistent.

After a few months of dating, he started taking her out to bars and introducing her to his circle of friends. She felt safe with him, so allowed herself to indulge in drugs and alcohol for the first time in her life—another change she'd let happen without a second thought. Adam took her to a party at one of the local frat houses one night. There, she met Blake. He was tall and handsome and offered her a drink, which Celia took after Adam insisted that his friends could be trusted. Just one drink. The next morning, she woke up in a haze, unsure of where she was or what had happened. She found herself lying naked in a strange bed. The whole room smelled of sex and weed. A tripod sat in the corner. She felt her heart sink at the realization of what had happened. That's when Blake and Adam walked in from the hallway, both smiling and pointing at the tiny screen of Blake's cellphone.

Her first instinct was to run—to get as far away as she possibly could and never look back, but that was never going to happen. Blake turned the phone toward her and showed her the video he'd made. He laughed aloud as Celia hugged her knees in the bed and cried.

"Oh no, don't look away baby, here comes the money shot." Blake said teasingly.

"Delete that now!" She demanded, but they refused.

Adam sat next to her and put a hand on her leg. She flinched, but his grip was firm.

"Here's what's going to happen, sweetheart," Celia turned away from him, but he grabbed her by the chin and forced her to face him. "You'll stay here for a few nights and entertain some of my friends, okay? You can drink, get high—have fun with it, but you're going to do what they tell you to, or this video we made last night is going to make its way to the internet, your parents, friends, your little sister, everyone. Do you understand that?"

Celia felt trapped. All she wanted was to take the last couple of months back and do things over—to pay closer attention to all those little changes, but it was too late for that. She couldn't let her family suffer the embarrassment of her poor decisions, so she agreed. After a month of being passed around the frat house, a new girl was brought in, the same way she had been. Once that girl was broken and compliant, Blake allowed Celia to leave, but only under his terms. He handed her the business card of one of his father's associates in the real estate banking business and a one-way bus ticket to New York.

"Look this guy up. He's fucking rich, and he'll take care of you—give you a job, set you up in an apartment. You'll have a good life and your parents won't be the wiser. Hell, they'll think you hit the jackpot. Just make sure you do whatever he says, okay? You know what'll happen if you don't."

Celia took the ticket and left, never looking back. New York had to be better than what she'd just endured. Now, seven years later, sitting at the reception desk of Tanner Greene's office, she knew she couldn't have been more wrong.

"Mr. Greene will see you now," Celia said without looking up.

Mike heard a faint buzz as she pressed the button on her desk, allowing him inside. He paused momentarily before walking in and handed Celia a handkerchief from the breast pocket of his suit. He said nothing, but Celia took the handkerchief and whispered, "Thank you," before Mike continued inside.

Moretti knew himself. He knew his livelihood depended on a certain level of brutality and that his job was to eliminate problems for other people then look the other way and keep his mouth shut. He provided those services to the highest bidder, and Greene was by far the highest, but he didn't like seeing innocent people hurt. Especially Celia.

Mr. Greene stood by the large office windows overlooking mid-town Manhattan. Rivulets of rain slid down the panes of glass as Tanner studied the busy streets below. Moretti had always thought the city to be more beautiful at night, and it appeared Tanner did as well.

"Have a seat, Mr. Moretti," Greene said before turning around.

Mike took the chair closest to the corner, giving him an unobstructed view of Mr. Greene, the windows, and the exit.

"It's late, Mr. Greene. I'm assuming we have a problem?"

"That we do, Michael."

Moretti cringed at the name. Only his mother, God rest her soul, had ever called him Michael.

"It's just Mike, sir."

"Well. Mike." Greene said as if the name left a sour taste in his mouth. "I need you to go to Richmond for me."

"Virginia?" Mike asked, surprised. He'd never been asked to leave the city on business. Mr. Greene never went anywhere except his office, the penthouse, or the occasional retreat to his sprawling estate in the Catskill Mountains.

"Yes. There, you'll link up with a man named JC Wilks, an associate who ran into a bit of trouble down south with a trade route." Tanner preferred the term trade to trafficking, but Moretti knew what he meant. "Take two of your men with you. I don't know what Mr. Wilks has planned, but I do know it may involve removing any obstacles to the new route we've tried to establish."

Mike was growing impatient. "Mr. Greene," he interrupted. "You know I'm a simple guy. I prefer straight talk over this—whatever this is, but I'm assuming you need me to meet this Wilks guy and kill whoever's interfering with the business. Am I right?"

Tanner frowned. He didn't like to speak so bluntly about the inner workings of his business. He found it to be crass and distasteful. Mike knew that but never missed an opportunity to make Mr. Greene feel uncomfortable.

"Yes, Michael. You are correct. Will that be a problem?"

"It's just Mike, sir, and no, that won't be a problem," Moretti said with more than a hint of malice in his voice. Greene paid well, but Mike knew that if it weren't for the money, Tanner would be the type of man he'd take pleasure in hurting. "I'll grab Vince and Franco. We'll head to Richmond first thing in the morning."

"Splendid," Tanner said as he turned back toward the windows.

Moretti stood to leave but paused by the door.

"Is there something else, Mr. Moretti?" Tanner asked without turning around.

"No sir," Mike paused before he continued, "but I couldn't help notice that somebody roughed up your secretary. I can look into that when I get back if you'd like me to."

Tanner knew the way he treated women bothered Mike but could care less about his feelings, "That won't be necessary, Michael," Tanner said, now facing Moretti.

The two men stared at each other silently before Tanner

broke eye contact and returned to his views of the rain-soaked city.

Mike walked out and stopped again at Celia's desk. He wanted to give her some reassurance that he could make the beatings stop. All she needed to do was ask, but he didn't want to cause the woman any further discomfort.

"Have a good night, Ms. Celia." He said as he walked back to the elevator.

As he turned back to press the button for the lobby, Celia looked up at him and smiled. Mike smiled back as the door closed quietly between them.

Chapter 9

After leaving the Sheriff's office, Case decided to take the long way home. It was good to be back in Pikesville and he wanted to take the extra time to reset his mind before reuniting with Sam. Big puffy clouds hung in the sky like floating versions of the white, blossoming cherry trees that dotted the surrounding landscape. Once past the city limits, Case noticed Bluebells and other wildflowers springing up along the fence lines. Mother cows grazed lazily among the green pastures as newborn calves bucked and played around them. Everything felt fresh and new—a reflection of Case's mood.

He pulled up at the farm to find Sam waiting patiently on the front porch with Dimpsey. But he barely made it out of the truck before being accosted by Trevor and Mia, who had been tossing a baseball back and forth in the yard.

"Case!" Mia exclaimed. "You're back."

"Yes, I am." Case said as he wrapped his arms around the girl. It felt like an eternity since the night he'd dropped her and Trevor off at the homecoming dance after the Grandview incident. She'd been through a lot in the weeks leading up to that night, but after everything that's happened, she seemed to be every bit as tough and strong-willed as her mother. Still, after what Bobby had told him, he had a hard time accepting her easy going attitude at face value and did his best to look a little deeper—beyond the smile.

Case put away his concerns and squeezed Mia tight, "I've missed you, girl. And I see you've been keeping an eye on this guy for me?" He said, looking over her head toward Trevor, who stood anxiously waiting for his turn.

Case let go of Mia and stuck his hand out. The boy seemed to have grown another six inches since they'd last seen each other. Trevor looked down at Case's hand and smiled.

"Really, she gets a hug and all I get is a handshake?" He said as he rushed in and wrapped his arms around the man he so admired.

Case felt Trevor's arms tighten and grunted. "Easy there, tiger. You'll crack a rib, and I still have more people to hug." He said with a strained laugh.

Sam and Dimpsey stood beaming from the porch rails. As Case walked up the steps, he took Dimpsey's large hand in his and, with the other, gripped the older man's shoulder. "It's good to see you again, Dimpsey. Thanks for keeping an eye on everything while I was gone."

"It was my pleasure, Case. We're all glad to have ya back."

Case then turned to Sam, who stood there looking as beautiful as ever. She wore straight-leg jeans over a pair of Anderson Bean boots, and a V-neck, short-sleeved t-shirt that showed off the newly formed and well-defined muscle in her arms. She looked stronger and more confident than he'd ever seen her, and that was saying a lot. Case stared at the big vertical scar that now sat prominently above her right eye—a remnant of the beating she'd taken from Rex Kelley the night Mia had been taken. He wanted to speak but couldn't. Sam knew he was struggling to put words to feelings, so she gently placed her hands on Case's cheeks and kissed him.

"You don't have to say anything now." She whispered softly in his ear. "We have the rest of our lives for that."

Case smiled and pulled Sam in close, inhaling deeply. Her

hair smelled like apples and mango. He'd missed her. "Yes, we do, Sam, and that starts tonight."

Everyone sat around the heavily laden table that evening, laughing and catching Case up on the latest happenings around town. Since Sam had moved in, she'd made a few changes to how meals were shared in the house. Gone were the days of eating on the couch in front of the television or crammed around the smaller table in the kitchen. To Sam, every meal shared with family and friends was a cause for celebration, so she preferred the more formal dining room that had only been used on holidays or special occasions when Case was a boy.

Since the meth operation in Grandview had been destroyed, things were finally returning to normal in Pikesville. Trevor informed Case that the Mustangs baseball team was finishing up spring training and was hopeful for a state championship. Trevor was being moved from center field to starting shortstop this year, and Case vowed to attend as many home games as he could. Business at the hardware store had been good. That's about all anyone was getting out of Dimpsey as he scraped a half-eaten biscuit around his plate before loading up with seconds. Bobby had worked diligently to get the sheriff's department back on track after everything that happened while Sam and Amanda finalized the wedding details.

The entire scene was perfect. After all these years of running away from the one thing he wanted most, Case took a moment to bask in the warmth of family and friends.

Bobby was the first to bring up Case's whereabouts over the past six months. "So, tell us about these folks you've been working with."

Case trusted his brother and would tell him anything, but he knew better than to discuss the CMP's classified projects with people outside the team, so he kept things honest but purposefully vague.

"Two of my former teammates from the FAMS left to do some contract work up north. The firm they work for specializes in things like human trafficking, so I went to them with the information I retrieved in Richmond. They pretty much handled everything from there."

"And I suppose you just sat on the sidelines and watched?" Sam asked skeptically.

"Not exactly." Case said, taking a renewed interest in the contents of his plate. He knew Sam wouldn't be pleased with the details of what had happened, so he didn't elaborate. Dimpsey saw the dissatisfaction in Sam's eyes and spoke up.

"Well, it's sure good to have ya back." He said, offering Case an escape from the conversation.

Case looked up and smiled at Dimpsey, who winked at him from across the table.

Sam watched the interaction and huffed. "OK, you two. Eat your chicken."

Chapter 10

Mike got to JC's apartment just as the sun began to set. Big purple clouds hung heavily against the red and gold hues of a half-lit sky. The James River Bridge stretched out in the distance. It reminded Mike of the Williamsburg Bridge that connected the lower east side of Manhattan to the Williamsburg neighborhood of Brooklyn where Mike had grown up.

Tanner hadn't been specific about what this job would entail, so he'd brought along two of his best men, Vincent and Franco. Both men were nationally ranked competitive shooters and fancied themselves as "gunslingers," but neither had ever fired a shot in combat, and they'd certainly never been shot at themselves. Vince was a former college athlete from Red Bank, New Jersey. He was fit and intelligent but had been kicked off the rowing crew at Princeton for assaulting a female student. Franco served as an Atlantic City vice cop for years but left after failing a random drug test. Mike had worked with them before. Both men were good at their jobs, but he knew they each still hid a sinister side. As did most of the people who worked for Mr. Greene. Although they weren't the caliber of men Mike had worked with in the past, they'd have to do. He was just thankful to have guys he didn't think would get him killed.

"Vince, you and Franco sit tight till I get back," Mike said as he exited the blacked-out Suburban.

Tanner's entire fleet of vehicles looked the same. Big black SUV's with darkly tinted windows, and heavy offroad tires. Greene felt the militaristic appearance lent an air of mystery and intrigue to his otherwise shady business. Mike knew it was all bullshit. Greene was just another man with money trying to intimidate the people around him. Moretti had spent years fighting alongside the men Tanner tried so hard to surround himself with—warriors, men of principle. But all Tanner had managed to accumulate was a sordid group of wannabe soldiers.

Mike thought back to his days in the SEAL teams. He was proud of what he'd accomplished there, but hated the way things turned out. He'd grown up in a rough part of Brooklyn and, like most boys in his neighborhood, turned to petty crime and violence as a means of climbing the social ladder. Joining the Navy was his way out. Once in boot camp, he found that he was good at the physical parts of training and looked for ways to push himself. When the Recruit Division Commander asked if anyone would like to take a shot at the SEALs, Mike volunteered for the BUD/S physical screening test and passed with flying colors. He landed in one of the winter classes, which was brutal, with already frigid water temperatures plunging into the lower 40's along the Coronado beaches. But once he got past hell week, Mike knew he'd make it to graduation. After several more months of the advanced SEAL Qualification Training, he received his trident along with eight other graduates.

He'd loved his job and the people he worked with, but once his mother was diagnosed with stage four breast cancer, Mike reverted to his old ways and started subverting the rules to help cover her medical expenses. It started small enough, taking unguarded gear from admin personnel and selling it—iPhones, watches, whatever he could get his hands on without drawing unnecessary attention. But what little money that generated wasn't enough to cover the bills back home and only made Mike feel crooked and dirty. That all changed one night after he and his team crashed an opium production plant on the outskirts of the Helmand Province. After the raid, Mike found himself alone in a room with enormous stacks of one-hundred-dollar bills, separated into currency straps of ten thousand apiece—money generated from the sale of poppy, which was, at the time, the country's most valuable commodity. It was more money than Mike had ever seen in his life—money that could help save his mother and get his life back on track.

The temptation was just too much. Mike pocketed five stacks of bills and walked away, thinking he'd never have to stoop so low again. Unfortunately, the intel officers who set the target up knew precisely how much currency was in that building. So, when they came up light after the count, a formal investigation was launched, and Mike was outed as a thief. After that, he was shunned by his fellow SEALs, court marshaled, and served five years in Leavenworth while his mother died alone in their tiny Brooklyn apartment. It was a disgrace. When he was released, he went back to the city he'd grown up in, but it wasn't the same. With no career, no family, and a pile of rapidly mounting debt, Mike took the executive protection position he'd heard about from an old teammate who still kept in touch. It paid well enough, but Mike had regretted the decision ever since. Now, Tanner used the things Mike had done in the course of his employment to keep him in check. That's how the man worked: through leverage, coercion, and blackmail and it's the reason no one on his security detail could be trusted—Greene had something on everybody. Mike knew that if he had the chance, he'd take what he could and disappear. Start over somewhere new, maybe a little place in the mountains far away from Tanner Greene and the city he'd grown to hate. Perhaps he could even talk Celia into coming with him.

Wilks answered the door in designer jeans and a half-buttoned shirt that probably cost more than Mike made in a week. A few months back, Franco had met JC during a meeting with Tanner and warned Mike that Wilks liked to think of himself as better than the people he worked for, but all Moretti saw now was another pretty boy who wanted to be something he wasn't.

"You must be Moretti," JC said, looking Mike up and down before turning away. "Come on in and shut the door behind you."

Mike did as he was told but felt an instant disdain for Wilks. The Rolex watch, five-hundred-dollar haircut, and luxury accommodations only highlighted the fact that he and JC couldn't be more dissimilar. Moretti also knew that, like most of his counterparts on the security team, JC liked to pretend. He'd come from a wealthy family and been educated at Wharton, but for some reason chose the company of bikers and thugs. Probably just to irritate his parents. Rich kids tended to do things like that. How both men had ended up in the same apartment together seemed impossible to Mike.

He looked around the richly appointed apartment and saw a girl sitting on the couch in front of a large gas fireplace. She was young, pretty, and smiled warmly when Mike walked in, but he could tell she was coming down from a prolonged high. Although she was wrapped in a heavy blanket, Mike could see her tiny frame trembling uncontrollably beneath it. He'd witnessed it a hundred times before while working for Mr. Greene. There was a pool of girls to choose from, and the ones they needed for specific purposes were sobered up and made presentable for public viewing, much like Celia. It was always hard to get them clean, but once they'd served their purpose, they were either sent back to the streets or never heard from again depending on their attitude. It was a cycle that Mike despised.

Moretti cut to the chase. "Mr. Greene says you need help with an issue down south."

"Yes, I do. How many men are with you?" JC asked.

"Two, both solid guys."

"Good. We're all going to take a little trip to Pikesville, Virginia. There's a man there I want dead. Are you and your men up for the job?" JC asked bluntly.

"That's what Mr. Greene pays us for."

"Well, Mr. Moretti, This is no ordinary man we're after. It's Case Younger. Do you know the name?"

"Sure. Federal Air Marshal, former Ranger. Stopped the first hijacking attempt since 9/11. Him and his guys were all over the news. Is that why you need the extra muscle?"

JC smirked. "Moretti, I would be more than willing to take this asshole out myself for what he did to me and my brothers, but—"

"You mean your little motorcycle gang?" Mike asked with more than a hint of sarcasm. He despised the flippant tone that men who'd never experienced actual combat took when they spoke about brotherhood or killing. Plus, it didn't take a genius to see that JC was worried about nobody but himself.

JC turned toward Mike. "Look here, tough guy. I know you work for Mr. Greene, but you're on loan to me right now, and I'm not just talking about killing Case. I'm talking about killing him in a way that makes him an example to others. I want every one of those hicks to understand that no one fucks with me or my business. If you think I'm just talking, or playing tough, then say one more goddamned word about my club and find out for yourself."

Moretti didn't move or back down. He disliked most of the people he worked with but tolerated their egos for the money. JC was no different.

"You're the boss."

"Good. We'll meet back here in the morning and head south. Once we get to Pikesville, we'll feel things out and come up with a plan. Until then, get your men settled for the night. I booked a room at the Richmond Marriott down the street. It's on my corporate account, but you'll need to give them your card for incidentals. I'm not paying for your booze or porn."

Mike said nothing. He just turned and left, leaving the door open behind him. He could already tell this was going to be a shitty assignment.

Chapter 11

Sam woke the following day with Case lying quietly beside her. She sat there for a while watching his chest rise and fall in the slow, steady rhythm of peaceful sleep. Her eyes traced the multitude of wounds covering his body— some were old, like the shrapnel scar on his right shoulder from an IED blast in Afghanistan and the bullet wound next to his neck from being shot the night he took down Rex Kelley's gang. Others were new, particularly the big yellowish bruise in the center of his sternum and the fresh scaring on his hands and knuckles. It was like piecing together a story. Sam loved Case but realized that, for now, it was best to let the man have his secrets. She worried about him though—worried about his anger and how it affected him. She hated seeing him struggle with it but knew it was something only he could fix. The question was, did he want it fixed?

Case had always been hot-tempered. But when he really lost it, like he did years ago, the night he beat up Jesse Williams at a bonfire party, his anger became focused and brutal to the point of being senseless. Case had changed a lot since then. In the twenty years he'd been away from Pikesville, he'd become more mature, confident, and controlled. But when the Dead Rebels kidnapped Mia, Sam witnessed firsthand what a man like Case could do when he was pushed too far. She remembered lying strapped to a gurney in front of the hospital when she told Case Mia had been taken. The rage she saw burning in his eyes that night was terrifying but measured and she was grateful to see it.

After they wheeled her away, she knew there wasn't a force on earth that would keep him from getting Mia back. A lot of men were dead as a result of what happened after that. But today, Mia was sleeping soundly down the hall, and Case was home at last. Sam pulled the sheet gently over Case's chest before kissing him on the cheek and slipping out of bed, certain that he needed the rest.

The mornings were still chilly this time of year in the Blue Ridge, so Sam wrapped herself in a thick robe and slid her feet into a pair of well-worn house shoes before walking down the hall toward the kitchen. She started a pot of coffee and stood in front of the sink, staring out the window toward the barn. It would be summer soon, and the back field needed a new fence to keep the cattle out. A chore she was sure Case would enjoy.

Sam started a small fire in the wood cook stove and rummaged through the cupboard for her flour and sifter. She didn't know where Case had been or what he'd been up to these past six months, but she knew she wanted him to feel at home when he woke up, and the best way to do that was to make him a big country breakfast like his mother, Molly, would have. Sam had never known the woman; Molly had succumbed to her battle with cancer well before she and Case had started dating, but Case had loved his mother and spoke of her often. When Sam moved into the old farmhouse, Case had made it a point to tell her where his mom's recipe box was—a not so subtle hint.

Before leaving for McLean to link up with Matt and Ross, Case had given Sam free reign to do as she pleased with the house. After restocking the cupboards, her first order of business had been to move Case's few belongings from the room he'd shared with Bobby as a child into the master bedroom. Mia had busied herself, settling into the smaller room while

Sam rearranged some furniture and added a fresh coat of paint to the living room, kitchen, and hallway. Looking around at the work she'd done, she was content. It made her happy to feel like a part of Case's life again, and now that he was home, she looked forward to the things they could do together.

As she sank her hands into the sticky biscuit dough, she heard Case coming down the hallway.

"What's all this?" He asked as he walked into the kitchen, wrapped his arms around Sam's waist, and kissed her cheek.

"You should still be sleeping, mister." Sam said as she kneaded the dough, "This was supposed to be a surprise."

Case released Sam and walked over to the coffee pot. "Sorry I blew it, but you know I can't resist the smell of freshly brewed coffee." He said as he retrieved his dad's old stoneware mug from its place on the counter and poured himself a cup.

"You've really spruced the place up in the last six months," Case mentioned as he looked around the kitchen.

"I just did a little painting and moved a few things around. Do you like it?"

Case sipped from his mug, "It looks great. This place was on the verge of collapse before you moved in."

"This place is just fine, and we'll continue to make it so," Sam replied with a grin. "Now, go get yourself cleaned up before breakfast. Bobby and Amanda wanted us to swing by the wedding venue later today."

"Yes, ma'am," Case said and he took his coffee and headed back down the hallway.

"And please wake Mia up for me," she yelled behind him.

Sam heard Case knock softly on Mia's door as he passed. "Mia, sweetheart. It's time to wake up."

The way he spoke to Mia always put a smile on Sam's face. It was gentle and sweet, unlike his normal, growly speaking voice. Sam started rolling out her biscuit dough content in the way things were turning out. This finally felt like home to her—a home she'd dreamt about since she was young and one she'd never let anyone threaten again.

Chapter 12

JC sped along I-64 West in his Red Audi R8, oblivious to the men in Tanner's black suburban trying to keep up. Prissy sat beside him, looking idly out the window as the world flew by in a blur of bright green dotted periodically by patches of white from the dogwood blossoms that lined the interstate. She would have been content if it hadn't been for the company she was keeping. This seemed to be the story of her life—letting men like JC take control while she just went along for the ride. Things needed to change. But at least now she could appreciate the scenery with a clear and sober mind.

She glanced in the side-view mirror and saw the Black SUV weaving in and out of traffic. She didn't have an opportunity to meet the two men who loaded her luggage in the trunk that morning, but the other one, Mike—the one in charge—she liked him. He projected an air of natural confidence that was absent in most of the men she knew. Mike seemed genuine, and he obviously irritated JC, which made things even more interesting.

"They still keeping up?" JC asked from the driver's seat.

"Yeah, they're still back there," Prissy responded dryly.

"What are you so down about?" JC asked. "Just think, after we get this done for Tanner, you're free and clear. You'll be able to go and do whatever you want. Hell, I'll even give you a little cash and let you keep the shit I bought you so you can get a fresh start. Doesn't that sound good?"

Prissy sat up and looked at JC, who smiled back at her. He was so charming. But she knew enough about men to understand that his kind of charm wasn't necessarily a good thing. It was an ability that took practice and was used to compel others into doing things they didn't naturally want to do. JC wielded his charm like a hammer and used it to hurt people like he did that old lady on Decatur Street. Prissy knew the game, and she knew better than to fall for it.

"That sounds great, JC."

JC shook his head and looked back at the road. Any other woman would have been happy to be in Prissy's position right now, but she acted like she had nothing to say about it. *How the hell did I end up with such a depressive little ingrate?*

"You know you could lighten the fuck up a little bit. This is all going to turn out great for you if you just do what you're told." JC lied. He had no intention of turning her loose. He'd spent way too long wallowing in that filthy house with the Rebels and girls like Prissy. The club was gone now, and it was finally time to make his way to the top. A loose end like Prissy could jeopardize that ascent, and there was no way he would let that happen.

As JC merged onto I-81 south toward Cook County, the scenery changed. The Shenandoah Valley spread out before him like a vast green ocean, with softly rolling hills surrounded by the taller blue mountains to the east and west, but the view was lost on him. His mind was singularly focused on eliminating Case Younger. JC glanced in his rear-view mirror and watched the black suburban struggling to keep pace. At least he had his sacrificial lambs tagging along. If this all went the way he envisioned, he'd be returning to Tanner alone, Case would be dead, and he could finally take his place at the head of the table where he belonged. JC smirked as he eased onto the gas and watched the black suburban sink further into the distance.

Chapter 13

Case sat in the passenger seat of Sam's blue Jeep Wrangler as they made their way to the Maple Grove Golf Resort, Cook County's premier outdoor wedding venue. It was a beautiful spring day in the mountains of Virginia and warm enough to have the top off. Sam's hair blew wildly around her face as the pair turned right off the Blueridge Parkway into the secluded gravel lot. Bobby and Amanda stood by the lake, which sat nestled against the eighteenth hole, holding hands. Amanda turned when she heard the car and waved them down.

"This is it, Sam," Amanda squealed as Case and Sam stepped out of the Jeep. "This is where we'll say our vows. The two women hugged as Amanda continued. "Then over there will be where we take the wedding photos. I was able to book Jake, the guy who does all the pictures for the historical society. He's so talented. Then the reception will be in the clubhouse. Oh my God, you have to see it —"

Sam and Amanda wandered across the meticulously cut grass toward the clubhouse and banquet hall, discussing their plans for the perfect wedding day, completely forgetting that Case and Bobby were standing beside them. The two men looked at each other and smiled.

"Are you ready for this, little brother?" Case asked.

"Case, I've been ready for this woman for a long time. I can't see spending my life with anyone but her."

"You did good Bobby. I'm proud of you."

Bobby looked out across the lake. "So now that we're

finally alone and have a little time, you want to tell me about Richmond?"

"You think me telling you what happened is a good idea?"

"We're brothers, Case. Let me help."

Case knew Bobby was right. He needed to unburden himself of what he'd done, and the best place he could think of to do that was with Bobby. After everything she'd been through, he wasn't ready to tell Sam yet, but he promised himself he would when the time was right.

"Alright." Case started, "When I got to Richmond, I tracked the Dead Rebels, watched them, established their patterns. I knew their routine, where they would be and how to hit them all at once. But I didn't know what was inside their headquarters until I got there."

"That's where they were hiding the girls?"

"Yeah, and it's where I found Tammy Lynn, the girl from Pikesville." Case paused, his eyes now distant and unfocused. "Fourteen years old Bobby. Some of those girls weren't even old enough to have a driver's license. They were scattered around that filthy house like dirty laundry—beaten and hopeless."

"What happened?"

Once I got into the house, I found some files…"

"What happened to the bikers, Case?"

Case looked his brother in the eyes. His gaze instantly more intense. "You get to ask me this once, Bobby, then I never speak of it again."

"Fair enough."

"I lost my temper. Seeing those girls like that—I never wanted to see anything like it again."

"What did you do?"

"I followed five bikers to a bar down the street from where

the girls were. I knew only the officers were inside, so I chained the doors and burned the place to the ground."

"Jesus Christ, Case," Bobby said, shaking his head.

"You were every bit as affected by this as I was, Bobby, and you've got two bullet holes in you to prove it. These men came after the people we love. I just wanted it over."

Bobby could never be as cold, or pitiless as Case, but understood his brother's reasoning. "What kind of files did you find in the house?"

"They'd been keeping records of the people who helped with the trafficking operation. I knew I couldn't take them all on alone, so I reached out to my friends at the CMP and handed everything over to them. They brought me into the operation, and we took the rest of them down legally."

"And it's done now?"

"It's over, Bobby. I just want to put all this behind me. I want to be left alone, and I want to be here for my family. That's it."

Bobby thought about his brother's situation for a moment. He knew Case had been through a lot in the months before coming back to Pikesville—the hijacking, the loss of his partner, Rebecca, and his decision to leave the Federal Air Marshal Service. He knew what his brother was capable of when he was angry, but he also knew Case would grow to regret his actions if he lost sight of the good he had done.

"Well, I guess there is a silver lining to all this."

"Yeah, and what would that be?"

"That little girl, Tammy Lynn she's back home now. Her mom cleaned herself up and her dad came back into the picture when he heard what happened. They have Tammy in counseling and they're trying to work things out. Amanda knows a few of her teachers and from what she says the girl's grades are good and she seems to be doing well at school. That's something, Case, and none of it would have ever happened if it hadn't been for what you did."

Case put a hand on his brother's shoulder. He knew what Bobby was doing and he was grateful for it. "Thanks, little brother."

"Just do me a favor, okay?"

"Anything." Case agreed.

"From here on out, you don't go at things like this alone. Nobody wants to see you get hurt."

Case agreed. "Hopefully, neither of us will have to deal with anything like that again. Settling down to a quiet life here in Pikesville suites me just fine."

"Good." Bobby said, "Now, let's go find the girls before Amanda decides to rent out the London Symphony Orchestra and a choir of angels."

Case laughed, "You go ahead," he said, watching his brother walk away. "I'll be right there."

Once Bobby was out of sight, Case dug around in his pocket and found the small, flower-shaped bullet that had struck him in the chest during his last op with the CMP. He turned it over in his hand, studying the sharp, lethal petals surrounding the heavy lead center. Just three inches higher, it would have missed the ballistic panel of his vest and ended Case for good. The thought of not being around anymore troubled him. He'd missed out on a lot over the years and wanted nothing more than to spend the rest of his life living peacefully with the people he loved. The bullet represented a part of his life that needed to be put behind him. Case clutched the small projectile in his hand, tossed it into the lake, and walked away.

Chapter 14

The Pikesville Motor Lodge was a relic from the past, built in 1956—the same year Dwight D. Eisenhauer signed the Federal-Aid Highway Act into law and began construction on the American Interstate system. For almost two decades, the one-story brick building had served as a stopping point for weary travelers traversing the Blue Ridge Mountains on their way to more temperate climates. But since the Virginia section of Interstate 77 was completed back in 1975, Pikesville had seen a steep falling-off in visitors. The Motor Lodge's interior décor naturally reflected that decline.

JC and Prissy stood in the center of their small 70s-style accommodations feeling as if they'd stepped back in time. It was clean and quaint, but JC couldn't stop complaining.

"Jesus, is this the only place to stay in this shithole town?" JC asked as he surveyed their new surroundings—an old brass bed was backed-up against a wood-paneled wall, a small table with two wicker-backed chairs sat beside the window facing the street, and a television set that had seen better days rested on a long laminate dresser across from the bed.

"I think it's cute," Prissy said as she wandered into the bathroom. "It feels…homely."

"You know that word means ugly, right?" JC said, throwing his leather bag on the bed.

Prissy huffed.

"But I guess it'll do till this Pikesville shit is over, so make yourself comfortable."

They could hear Mike and his men getting settled in the adjoining room and decided to do the same. JC watched as Prissy unpacked her new Versace bag and held up the things he'd bought her. The entire wardrobe had only cost a couple grand at Verdalina's on Broad Street, but Prissy admired each piece as if it were made for a queen. It wasn't that JC gave a shit about how she looked, but she'd be posing as his fiancé and couldn't be seen around town dressed like a common whore.

Prissy was the last remnant of the old Richmond operation and, after JC got her out of jail, had been instrumental in identifying Case Younger as the man who'd freed the other girls and knocked off JC's club. Case had also stolen the files they kept on everyone who helped move the girls and used that information to dismantle the entire business from the ground up, but the destruction stopped short of Mr. Greene. Greene was no fool. There was no file on him for Case to find. Now Greene needed Case dead to tie up that loose end before rebuilding. JC planned on using Prissy one last time to help make that happen. Then she'd be found dead of an overdose somewhere, perhaps in a gas station bathroom like a lot of women in her position. No one would give the girl a second thought.

"I'm going to go for a drive. Tell the guys to park that suburban in the back and rent something we can all fit in. A vehicle like Tanner's may draw attention around here."

"Sure thing, JC." She said with a smile. Prissy knew she needed to stay compliant if she expected to survive this. "I'll tell them. Is there anything else I can do while you're gone?"

"Just keep quiet and don't leave this motel unless I say so. I have some people I want to introduce myself to."

Prissy watched from the window as JC pulled away in the bright red Audi, a car that costs three times the average annual salary in a place like this. *And he thinks a black SUV will draw attention? It's a good thing he's handsome.* She said to herself as she went back to unpacking her pretty new things, happy to finally have a clear mind and some time alone.

JC had the address of the Younger farm but knew better than to approach Case head-on. The man was obviously dangerous. Nonetheless the only way JC could move up within the ranks of Mr. Greene's organization was to eliminate Younger. JC also needed to set an example. He wanted the town of Pikesville to witness what happens when they fuck with his business and the best way to do that would be to have the people closest to Case watch him die for what he'd done—to see the consequences of their actions played out in front of them. He just needed to figure out who those people were. JC already had a picture of the truck Case used the night of the fire. Detective Donaldson had given him the rest. The address, known acquaintances, which weren't many, and a picture of the other truck registered in Case's name. A flat gray 2021 Dodge Ram 2500. Plate number ADL-97E. JC sat in the Dollar General parking lot on the corner of Route 58 and Main. He knew that if Case came through town, he'd be coming this way. Their meeting had to look like a chance encounter. Patience would be critical.

He was just cracking open his third Red Bull when he saw the big gray Dodge sitting at one of the town's two red lights, signaling right toward Main Street. "Finally, some good luck." He quickly downed the drink and pulled out slowly, careful not to get too close. JC followed the truck down Main to the local hardware store situated at the end of a long row of connected brick buildings and waited, but Case wasn't the one driving. It was a kid. The boy jumped down from the driver's seat, wearing a dirty blue and gold baseball uniform, with a ballcap covering thick, curly brown hair. Case was nowhere in sight. JC sat and watched as the kid walked inside, waited a few minutes, then followed.

Campbell's Hardware was from a bygone era. Absent were the appliances and power tools associated with modern home improvement chains. Instead, the shelves were lined with spools of barbed wire and fencing staples, assorted hand tools, and the basic components one might need to keep a modest farm in good working order. JC looked around to see the boy he'd followed inside talking excitedly to an older man behind the counter. Two more men who looked to be in their seventies played checkers at a rickety wooden table in the corner. Everyone turned to look at the newcomer.

"Hello there, stranger," The old man said from behind the counter, "What can I help ya with?"

JC had to think quickly. The boy had been driving Case's truck, so there had to be a connection. He looked at the boy's uniform and settled on his approach, "Well, sir. I just got into town with my fiancé and a couple of coaches from up north. I'm unfamiliar with the area and was wondering if you could tell me how to get to the high school."

"I just came from the high school," The boy offered, "Are you gonna be the new gym teacher?"

JC turned on the charm and laughed as if he gave a shit about the boy or his gym teacher. "No, son, I'm not, but I believe I may have come to the right place. I'm a baseball scout for the University of Maryland." He said, improvising freely now. "I've been sent down here to evaluate players from some of the regional high school teams. It looks like you may be one of the kids I'll be watching. What's your name?"

"No way!" Trevor exclaimed, "My name's Trevor Campbell."

"Oh, like the sign outside?" JC asked, pointing over his shoulder.

"Yes, sir. This is my grandpa's place."

Dimpsey eyed the man suspiciously as he did most strangers, then walked around the counter and stuck his hand out. "Hi, I'm the boy's grandpa, Dimpsey Campbell. I didn't catch your name."

JC liked to establish dominance up front, so he took the man's hand and squeezed hard. He was shocked when the old guy matched his grip, then gave a little extra just for good measure. He wasn't expecting someone of his age to be so strong. A little embarrassed, JC accepted the pain and managed to keep the smile on his face. "My name is JC Wilks." He said through clenched teeth, "It's a pleasure to meet you."

"And you're in town scouting ball players?"

"Yes, sir. We've gone a couple of years without a championship, so the university's starting to put more emphasis on recruiting with the hopes of taking a title within the next three seasons." JC said, pulling his hand away from the old man.

"Well," Dimpsey said, walking back around the counter. "You've come to the right place. Our Mustangs have always had a hell of a team. As a matter of fact, Trevor here will be starting shortstop for the Mustangs this year."

JC feigned interest when he saw an opportunity to inquire about Case. "Is that right? I guess I'll definitely be keeping an eye on you then. Judging by the truck you pulled up in, I assumed you were a pro already. Is that your grandpa's?"

"Oh, no. That was a gift from my friend Case. We're neighbors."

"Well, that's some friend you have there."

"You don't know the half of it, mister. Case is—"

"Trevor," Dimpsey interrupted, "Shouldn't you be getting back to the farm? You have feeding to do before supper, and I want you washed up when you sit at my table."

Trevor looked crestfallen, "Okay, Grandpa. It was nice to meet ya, Mr. Wilks. I hope to see ya at the game Wednesday night." He said as he left.

JC watched through the painted window as the boy climbed back into the truck and pulled away.

"Well, gentlemen," JC said, nodding to the two unsmiling old-timers sitting in the corner. Neither man had touched a checker since he'd walked in. "I suppose I should get going as well. I appreciate your time."

JC rushed back to the parking lot just as Trevor drove out of sight. He'd found a way to get close to Case but was so hurried to get back to the hotel he didn't think to get directions to the high school—a minor detail. He was certain no one had noticed.

Chapter 15

Trevor couldn't wait to get back home and tell Case about his run-in with the scout. After sprinting anxiously around the house, he found Case by the barn working under the hood of his dad's old pickup.

"Case, you're never gonna believe what happened," Trevor shouted as he rounded the corner.

The sudden interruption startled Case, causing him to bang his head. "Whoa, buddy. What's all the excitement about?" He asked as he rubbed the back of his skull.

"I was just at the hardware store and ran into a baseball scout from the University of Maryland. He's gonna be at my next game."

"That's fantastic news. When's that?"

"Wednesday at 5:00 p.m. Coach already said he was starting me, so—" Trevor stopped.

"What's the matter?"

"What if I screw up, Case?"

Case considered the question thoughtfully. "Look, Trevor. You're a junior starting shortstop on the varsity team. That's pretty rare, but it speaks to your talent. You've been playing ball since you were five, so I'm pretty sure you're ready. You just play your best and support your teammates. I'm sure he'll be knocking on your door by senior year."

"You think so, Case?"

"I know so." Case said smiling and rubbing at the knot he

felt swelling on the back of his head. "And I'll be there to cheer you on."

"You're the best, Case. Sorry about your head." Trevor exclaimed as he took off sprinting toward the house, "Hey, Mia! Guess what?"

Mike sat at the small table by the window, reading the local paper when JC barged in. "Where are the guys?"

"They ran to the diner to pick up some food. What's up?"

JC banged on the adjoining wall. "Prissy, get your ass in here."

Prissy rushed in, looking concerned. "Jesus, JC, what's wrong?"

"Nothing's wrong. But I figured out how we can get to Case." JC walked over to the table where Mike was sitting and tore a piece of paper from the complimentary notepad. He grabbed a pen and started writing out a list of names.

> *Bobby Younger*
> *Samantha Raines*
> *Mia Raines*
> *Dimpsey Campbell*
> *Trevor Campbell*

He hadn't paid attention to it at the hardware store, but writing the last two names down triggered something in JC's memory. He felt like he'd heard those names spoken somewhere before. He didn't know when or where, but they definitely sounded familiar. JC pushed the thought aside and reviewed what he'd written before handing the list to Mike.

"What am I looking at here," Moretti asked.

"These are the people closest to Younger. They're the ones I need to witness what happens when someone crosses me."

Moretti studied the list, unimpressed with JC's pomposity. "We already knew about the brother, girlfriend, and little girl. Who are the other two?"

"I ran into them at the local hardware store. Trevor's just some teenager, but he was driving Case's truck and said they were friends. Dimpsey is the boy's grandfather—tough old bastard, but he has to be over seventy. They're neighbors with Case."

Again, that feeling of familiarity crept into JC's head.

Mike didn't like the idea of involving women and children but kept his feelings to himself. "Okay," Mike said, laying the paper on the desk in front of him, "So, how do you suppose we get this done?"

"I'll figure that out soon enough."

JC looked over at Prissy, "In the meantime, I need you to go out and buy some things. Mike and I will each need a pair of tan Dockers, a clipboard, some blank paper, pens, and a stopwatch. Then, get on my laptop and go to the University of Maryland's website. Order two polo shirts with their logo on them. We need those delivered here before Wednesday."

Prissy scratched out a list of her own, "Sure thing, JC, but what's all this for?"

"It's for the baseball game we're attending Wednesday night. Now stop asking so many fucking questions and get to work."

Chapter 16

Case and Dimpsey stood against a long stretch of new barbed wire fence surrounding the back thirty acres watching as large red and white Hereford cows grazed in the thick green grass. It had taken days, but the additional fence would keep the cattle out of the back field, allowing the grass on the other side time to grow and be cut for hay later in the summer. Being away for so long, Case had forgotten how much he enjoyed working around the farm. As a FAM, he'd hit the gym at least four days a week and always ran a few miles on the days he didn't lift. He'd consistently maxed his quarterly PT tests, even in the 18 to 21 age bracket, and considered himself to be in decent shape for his age, but there was nothing like digging a row of post holes to let you know just how out of shape you really were. Case walked over to the tractor, grabbed two ice-cold bottles of water from a small cooler strapped to the back, and tossed one to Dimpsey.

Both men sat with their backs against the fence row, relishing in the satisfaction of a hard day's work. Case broke the silence first. "So, Trevor tells us they'll be a scout at the game on Wednesday."

Dimpsey retrieved an old paisley handkerchief from his shirt pocket and wiped the sweat and dirt from his big hands.

"I've been meaning to talk to you about that," Dimpsey said after taking a long pull from the water bottle. "That boy's excited as all get out, but have you ever seen any college scouts in Pikesville before?"

"Not that I know of. Bobby was offered a scholarship to the University of Virginia his senior year, but I wasn't around then. So, there could have been one, I guess."

"This whole scout thing just strikes me as odd."

"How so?"

"I don't know. It just seemed strange to me that a college scout from Maryland would walk into the hardware store right behind Trevor and ask directions to the high school. Don't phones have GPS in 'em now?"

"Yes, they do, but maybe he doesn't get service here in the mountains. A lot of people complain about that."

"I suppose, but the man left right after Trevor did and never got the directions he came for in the first place. The whole thing just seemed strange."

Case considered Dimpsey's misgivings and filed them away in the back of his mind until he could learn more. "I told Trevor I'd be at the game Wednesday night. If you point the scouts out to me, I'll introduce myself and see what I can find out. Would that help put your mind at ease?"

Dimpsey nodded, "Yes, it would. I appreciate it, Case."

After downing their waters, the two men packed up their equipment and headed back toward the house. The sun was getting low on the horizon, and since returning home, Case liked to spend his evenings on the couch watching old movies with Sam and Mia. The baseball scout would have to wait till Wednesday.

Sam walked into the living room carrying two large bowls of popcorn. "Scooch over," she said as she slid between Case and Mia. "What are we watching tonight?"

"Sergeant York, with Gary Cooper." Case said as he shoved his hand into one of the bowls. The movie had always been one of Avis's favorites.

"What's it about?" Mia asked.

"It's about a hero from World War I who was reluctant to fight."

"Why was he reluctant?"

"He was from a small town in Tennessee, not far from here. When he was young, he was a bit of a wild man, drinking, fighting, and getting into trouble. But he found religion and decided he didn't want to fight anymore."

"But they sent him to war anyway?" Mia asked.

"His commander convinced him that sometimes war was necessary to protect the greater good. That some things are just worth fighting for."

"So, he fought?"

"Yes, he did, and it turns out he was pretty darn good at it. Now watch the movie." Case said as he tossed a piece of popcorn in her direction.

As the black and white Warner Brothers logo appeared on the small TV screen, Case turned to Sam.

"Hey, you and Mia are going to watch Trevor's game on Wednesday, right?"

Sam huffed, "Do you really think I could keep Mia away from one of Trevor's games?"

Case decided not to mention the scout or the suspicions Dimpsey was having. He didn't see the point in getting everyone riled up. "Good. It'll be fun to finally see the kid in action."

Chapter 17

Case had a hard time sleeping that night. Something felt off in Pikesville. He thought back to the CMP missions and dismantling the Dead Rebels trafficking chain. The team had followed the evidence and systematically taken away every function of the operation, effectively putting it to an end, but Case wasn't naive. He knew the people they'd removed were ground-level guys, easily replaced. There had to be someone else pulling the strings—the man behind the curtain. If that were the case, then the problem hadn't been stopped, only diverted, which didn't sit well with Case.

Unable to shut down his mind, Case slipped out of bed and into his jeans and flannel. He crept down the hall and onto the porch, quietly closing the door behind him. He stood in the cool night air for a while, pacified by the tranquil sounds of nature. Crickets, owls, and peep frogs chirping from the creek bank helped to relax his overactive mind, and in the distance, Case thought he could hear the faint melody of a familiar song. The soft strum of a guitar floated across the fields from Dimpsey's place—a comforting sound that reminded him of his childhood. Case slipped on his work boots, stepped off the porch and started walking down the long gravel drive toward the sound of *You Are My Sunshine*.

Dimpsey sat in his rocker, picking softly at his old guitar.

"You can't sleep either?" Case asked as he stepped onto the porch.

"Some nights are just better for thinkin' than sleepin', I suppose."

Case took a seat in the rocker next to Dimpsey. "Trevor's gone to bed?"

"Yeah, the boy's so damned excited, I think he finally wore himself down around ten."

Case chuckled, and the two sat quietly—content to share in the stillness as Dimpsey continued his melody.

"How are things since you got back?" Dimpsey asked.

"Good. Sam's done a lot since her and Mia moved in. The place looks great and they seem to be settling in."

Dimpsey stopped picking and looked at Case. "That's not what I meant."

Case looked across the yard toward the soft glow of his own porch light. "I know. I'm fine, Dimpsey. Really."

Dimpsey leaned back in his rocker and continued to pick at the guitar. "Ya know, it's not easy for some men to give up the fight."

"What do you mean?"

"I mean, some men are just built for conflict, and in the absence of it, they can get restless. That's usually not a good thing."

"Is that why you're sitting out here in the middle of the night, playing guitar?" Case asked.

Dimpsey leaned his guitar against the porch railing. "No, son. I gave up my fight a long time ago. Now, my worries tend to revolve more around other people. Like that boy I got sleeping inside there—and you."

"Me?"

"Yes, you. You know I've always looked at you and Bobby as my own. Bobby seems to be building something nice for himself around here, and I want the same thing for you and Sam. I just don't want to see you get in your own way and blow it."

"Why do you think I would do that?"

Dimpsey leaned forward. "Because you're your daddy's boy, through and through."

Case scoffed at the thought.

"You might not want to see it, but I do. Your daddy was a good man, Case. He was just broken. The war and his inability to separate himself from it did that to him."

"And you think the same is happening to me? That I can't separate myself from the fight?"

"Not necessarily. I know you want something different, but there's a restlessness to you now, son. You're gonna have to figure out a way to balance that."

"I think I can do that."

"Good. Because you've got a hell of a woman at your side now and a little girl who's depending on you to keep it together. They've been through a lot and deserve a life without all the conflict."

Case sat silently for a while. He thought about Sam and Mia, sleeping soundly back at the house. There was a life there that he'd always wanted. All he had to do now was accept it.

"You're right, Dimpsey. I can give them that."

Dimpsey smacked his palms onto his knees and stood. "Good. Your daddy would be proud of you, Case."

"Ya think so?"

The old man placed one big hand on Case's shoulder. "I know so. Now, let's both get some sleep. We've got the big game tomorrow." Dimpsey said as he opened the screen door and stepped inside.

"Ok. Good night, Dimpsey."

Case heard the door close behind him but he stayed, rocking in his chair, looking across the field toward his family home. That's what it was now, a home. Case stood and stepped off the porch into the darkness, letting the light guide him across the yard and back to Sam.

Chapter 18

Prissy met Mike at the ice machine under the covered vending area of the Pikesville Motor Lodge. He wore his new Dockers and Maryland Terrapins polo, looking very much like a college baseball coach—handsome and athletic. Prissy hadn't had an opportunity to speak to Mike alone, so she decided it was time to break the ice.

"Hey." She said shyly.

"Hey. It's Prissy, innit?" Mike asked as he studied the selection in the vending machine.

Prissy smiled at the man's thick Brooklyn accent. It reminded her of Robert DeNiro in *Taxi Driver*. "Priscilla, actually."

"Like the king's wife, right?"

"If you mean Elvis, then yes. My grandma saw him sing at a fair once, in Mississippi. I'm pretty sure if I'd been born a boy, my name would be Elvis instead of Priscilla."

"Well, it's a lovely name. My mother was a big fan too."

"Who wasn't, right?"

"Right." In the silence that followed Mike considered asking the girl how she'd gotten tangled up with a man like JC but thought better of it. Who was he to judge? "You excited about the ballgame this evening?"

"I'll just be happy to leave that room and feel like a normal person for a change."

Prissy's blond hair shone like silk in the bright sunlight. Mike couldn't help himself. He had to know. "You and JC an item?"

Prissy was shocked. "Me. No, I'm just a—"

"It's none of my business anyway." Mike said, cutting her off. He knew good and well what the girl was to JC but didn't want her to feel embarrassed.

Mike pressed two buttons on the vending machine, regretting the question, and waited silently for his Payday bar to drop. "I should get back to the room. You have a good evening, Ms. Priscilla."

Prissy watched as Mike walked away. He seemed nice, but she'd been around enough men to know the dangerous ones when she saw them, and Mike was most definitely a dangerous man.

Mike turned and spoke again before walking into his room. "You could just leave, ya know."

The look on Priscilla's face was almost sympathetic. She'd known a few men like Mike in the past, the rescuers, as she called them. Men who saw women in bad situations and wanted to help without expectations of anything in return. It was a noble trait, but pointless none the less. "No, Mike, I can't. But thank you for believin' that of me."

Chapter 19

The Cook County ballfield lay warming under the late April sun as spectators paid their five-dollar admission and filtered through the chain link entrance. They filed into the metal bleachers and lined up at the concession stand, chatting happily about the team's chances of a state championship this year. There was always an air of excitement surrounding the opening day of Mustangs baseball, but today was extra special. Trevor would be starting shortstop, and somewhere in that ever-growing sea of blue and gold, there was a scout from the University of Maryland. Dimpsey had doubts about the man, but Case was excited to introduce himself and put in a good word for Trevor.

"There's Trevor!" Mia pointed as the players made their way onto the field for the warmups.

Trevor jogged past, grinning wildly, and waved back to Mia.

"Any sign of the scout yet?" Sam asked.

"Nothing yet. But Dimpsey here will point him out when he shows up. Besides, we don't want to bum-rush him as soon as he walks in the gate. We need to play it cool for Trevor."

Sam agreed, and after buying a few hotdogs and a strip of 50/50 tickets from the roving vendor, the four took their seats in the bleachers and waited patiently for the game to start.

The first inning was relatively uneventful. The Mustangs pitcher, Colton Hobbs, threw flawlessly, sitting down three Pulaski Cougars in a row. At bat, the Mustangs managed to get on base but couldn't hold the momentum. Things got a little more exciting in the second inning. With a man on second, the Cougars hit a groundball double into left field, sending one runner home, but the Mustangs answered with two singles and a home run, making the score 3 to 1, Mustangs.

In the third inning, Trevor faced off against the Cougars starting pitcher Jarod Grimes, who was known to have a wicked inside curveball. Trevor hadn't seen the pitch all evening and knew it was due. Jared started his windup from the mound and sent the ball screaming toward home plate. Trevor watched as the pitch came directly at him, threatening to knock him out of the batter's box, but he stood his ground. As the pitch started to drop and curve toward the outside edge of the plate, Trevor swung. The crack of the bat sent the crowd into a frenzy. The ball flew high over center field and, at its apex, seemed to hang there, suspended by some unseen hand. Everyone watched breathlessly as the centerfielder lined himself up, using his glove to shield his eyes from the late-day sun. After what felt like forever, the ball fell toward the ground.

"He dropped it!" Mia screamed as Trevor sprinted around first base, heading toward second. The embarrassed centerfielder scooped the ball up and launched it toward third to hold Trevor at second. Everyone stood and cheered as Dimpsey nudged Case in the ribs.

"That's him," Dimpsey said, nodding toward the entrance.

Case turned his attention to two men and a woman standing between the dugout and concession stand.

The men wore khakis and polo shirts with the University of Maryland logos embroidered on the chest. One was tall and lean, with slicked-back blond hair and expensive sunglasses. He had a stopwatch hung around his neck and carried a clipboard.

The other man was shorter and built more like a football player, bald with broad shoulders and a thicker midsection. He looked on edge as his head moved back and forth, scanning the crowd. *This guy looks more like security than a baseball scout,* Case thought to himself.

The woman with them was young and pretty. She had long blond hair pulled into a ponytail and wore a light-yellow sun dress that reminded Case of his mother. Maybe that's why she seemed so familiar. She looked genuinely excited to be at the game, smiling brightly and greeting the people around her.

"Do you think they saw Trevor's hit?" Mia asked.

Case watched as the scouts took a seat at the end of the bleachers closest to the exit. If he wanted to talk to the guy, he'd have to catch him before the end of the game, or he'd be gone.

"I'll tell ya what. Let them get settled in and watch a few more innings. Then, I'll head to the concession stand and say hello. Sound good?"

Dimpsey nodded, and Mia beamed with excitement. Case sat back down beside Sam and looked across the field toward the parking lot. Two more men stood along the right-field fence. Both wore jeans, untucked shirts, and wrap-around sunglasses. Something in the way they held themselves put Case on edge.

Case leaned over to Dimpsey. "You recognize those two?" He asked, indicating the men at the fence.

"Never seem 'em before."

"Maybe they're with the away team." Case said as he returned his attention to the game. He didn't really believe they were with the opposing team, but he didn't want to raise Dimpsey's suspicions any further. He'd make it a point to keep an eye on the two men.

By the start of the fifth inning, the score was 5-4, with the Mustangs still ahead. Mia stood and cheered as Trevor took the field again. After four at bats, Hobbs struck two out but allowed two singles in between, putting runners on first and second. Now, to the dread of every Mustang on the field, the Cougar's star hitter, Don Witley, stepped up to the plate.

"Look at Hobbs." Dimpsey said, pointing, "That boy's shaking so bad he's about to come out of his shoes."

"Jesus, Dimpsey. You'd be nervous in his position, too," Sam said from the edge of the bleachers.

"I suppose I would."

Hobbs started his windup and let loose with a fastball. Witley swung hard, and connected, the ball took a wild hop between the pitcher and third baseman. Trevor sprang immediately to his right and dove, outstretched toward the ball. He managed to stop it and, in a cloud of dust, rose to one knee, tossing the ball to third just as the runner crossed.

"You're out!" The ump screamed as the crowd stood and cheered. Case and Dimpsey were ecstatic, screaming and applauding excitedly. Trevor was having an amazing game. Case looked over at the scout. The man didn't cheer or make notes on his clipboard, and he certainly wasn't looking at the field. Instead, his head was turned toward the crowd, searching. Maybe it was his imagination, but it looked as if the man paused when his eye's crossed Case. The scout then turned casually back the game and clapped along with everyone else.

"Do you think now would be a good time to go introduce yourself to the scout?" Mia asked.

Case stared at the men from Maryland. An uneasy feeling sat like a stone in the pit of his stomach, "Yes, sweetheart. I think it is."

Chapter 20

Mike stood as Case strode toward their seats in the bleachers. Just as Case was about to speak, he stuck out his hand.

"Mister Younger, how do you do?"

The introduction threw Case off. "I'm sorry, do we know each other?"

"I apologize, sir. My associate here, Mr. Wilks, spotted you in the crowd." Mike nodded toward the other man. "He pointed you out, and I couldn't let you pass by without saying hello. It's a real pleasure to meet you."

Case shook the man's hand and glanced at Wilks, who looked up without speaking. The woman at his side smiled nervously in his direction. Case couldn't shake the feeling he knew her from somewhere but couldn't make the connection.

"So, you guys are scouting for Maryland?"

"Yes, sir. We have our eyes on a few kids from the region. No one in particular from either of these teams, but since we were in the area, we figured we'd catch a few games—see what was there, ya know? You got a kid on the field?"

Case started to relax. "Me, no. I'm here for my neighbor's grandson. He's the kid playing short."

"Talented kid. That was a hell of a play he just made. Are his folks around?"

"It's just his grandpa now, but he's here." Case looked over his shoulder toward Dimpsey and pointed with his thumb. "He's the one you can hear cheering over everyone else." Case said, shifting his attention to the other man. "Your friend here ran into him at the hardware store the other day. Trevor knew you guys would be at the game, so I promised him I'd introduce myself."

JC wasn't paying attention. His eyes were locked on Trevor, who stood in the dugout, celebrating with his teammates. Mike saw that JC's mind was elsewhere so he kept control of the conversation, "My apologies. This is my boss, JC Wilks, and his fiancé, Priscilla Reynolds. Mr. Wilks, this is the man you were telling me about."

JC turned and extended his hand. "I'm well aware. I apologize for staring earlier, Mr. Younger. I recognized you from the news, and, well, it's a pleasure to finally meet you in person."

Case took the man's hand and felt him squeeze a little too hard. His dad, Avis, had always taught him that a handshake wasn't a power struggle. It was two people showing mutual respect for one another. *Any man that tries to overpower you during a handshake is an asshole, son.*

"The pleasure is all mine." Case said with a forced smile.

"You say the boy's mother isn't around anymore?" JC asked, pointing toward Trevor.

"I didn't, but no, she's not."

JC realized his mistake. "My apologies. It's just that I knew a girl named Campbell who I think might have been from around here. But that was a long time ago."

Case eyed the man suspiciously. "Well, it's a pretty common name around here."

JC feigned as if he'd had an epiphany, "Ya know—now that I think about it, I believe she might of been from around Blacksburg somewhere," He was lying of course. JC knew exactly who the boy's mother was and where she was from. Now he realized why the names had sounded so familiar to him at the hardware store.

"So, how long will you guys be in town?"

JC didn't answer, but instead turned his attention back to Trevor, his mind still processing the unlikely connection.

Mike jumped in again hoping that JC would snap out of it. "Oh, just long enough to catch a couple of games and evaluate the local talent. A couple of weeks, maybe. This is really a beautiful place." Mike said, turning the subject away from baseball. "I'm originally from Brooklyn and always dreamed of a little spot like this—fresh air and mountains. You're a lucky man."

There was a sincerity about Mike that made him likable, and Case recognized something else in the man that most people might have missed. "What branch did you serve in, Mike?"

Mike had always been ashamed of what he'd done and how his career ended, but he was still proud of his service and the men he'd fought alongside. "Navy, SEAL Team Five. How did you know?"

"You just have that look, and please call me Case."

"Case it is then." Mike said smiling. "You were in the—"

"I know this may seem a little premature," JC interrupted suddenly. "But we'd love to sit down and talk to Trevor about his goals moving forward. Nothing too serious, just a get-to-know-ya kind of thing. Do you think we could make that happen?"

Case was stunned by the offer and knew everyone would be ecstatic, but something still felt off about JC. He needed time to think things through.

"I'll tell ya what. Trevor's an excitable kid. I'll tell him and his grandpa you'd like to sit down and chat, but he'll need a minute to get himself under control. How about we all meet for breakfast at the diner on Saturday morning around 9:00.

Does that work for you?"

"Sure thing," JC said. We'll see you then."

"Perfect. I'll let everyone know."

With that, the three men shook hands again. Case made eye contact with JC's fiancé and nodded politely before continuing to the concession stand. When he returned, JC, Mike, and the woman were gone. As were the two men who had been standing by the fence.

———

"What the fuck was that?" Mike asked JC as they all made their way back to the off-white Chevy Blazer Franco had rented.

"What are you talking about, Mike?"

Mike knew of JC's reputation but found it hard to tolerate incompetence.

"That." Mike said pointing back toward the ballfield. "What just happened back there? This is your fucking operation. You're the one who came up with this baseball scout bullshit to get close to Case. Now, when you're finally right in front of the guy, you freeze up. Are you trying to get us blown? Because trust me, This Case fella' isn't a man you want to take lightly."

JC stepped aggressively toward Mike, "I suggest you watch the tone you take with me, Moretti. You don't know who you're fucking with."

"Oh, don't I?" Mike stopped in front of JC and turned toward him. Prissy could see the situation escalating and backed away. Vince and Franco did the same. "I know enough to know you're nothing more than a trust fund baby who decided to show Mommy and Daddy he was a real man, so you started living the thug life with that fuckin' little gang of yours to prove a point."

JC's fists clenched at the comment. "You watch your fucking mouth, Mike."

Mike didn't back down. "You're the one with the bright idea of killing Case to prove some god damned point. We could get this shit done right now and walk away clean if you weren't bein' so fuckin' dramatic about it."

"This is my show, Moretti. Mine!" Wilks said, stepping even closer to Mike. "Mr. Greene put you and your men on loan to me. So, you do what I tell you, or so help me God, I won't stop at Case. Do you understand me?"

Mike knew when to back off. He'd made his point. "Sure. But I'll tell you this. I'll do whatever needs to be done to shut Case down so I can get paid and wash my hands of this shit. But that's all you're getting from me. You can handle the rest however you see fit. You got a problem with that; take it up with Mr. Greene."

Mike turned and walked away with Vince and Franco, leaving JC alone with Prissy. He'd let this go for now. As the three men climbed into the rental, JC stood watching, his thoughts shifting back to Trevor and his mother, Tina.

JC recalled Rex Kelley bringing the grief-stricken woman up to Richmond shortly after her husband had died. Rex wanted her under the Rebel's protection but never explained why. She'd shown up strung out on meth and batshit crazy to boot but still good-looking enough to turn a trick for the club. As soon as Rex headed south again, a few of the guys went to work trying to recruit her. She was reluctant, but with enough incentive, she could be flipped. JC remembered her getting high at the Rusty Spoke and chattering away about returning home to the mountains and her little boy Trevor. That's why the name sounded so familiar. He didn't think the knowledge of Tina's whereabouts could help him get closer to Case, so he'd keep that to himself until he knew how to leverage the information. He needed to find an alternative approach.

"Prissy, I need you to do something for me."

"Sure, JC." She replied nervously.

"Did you see that woman Case was with?"

"Yeah."

"Find a way to get close to her. We need to come at this from a different angle."

Mike sat in the rented Blazer without speaking and watched JC and Prissy as they talked in the parking lot. JC was animated and visibly heated while Prissy stood with her head down, taking whatever abuse he was dishing out. Mike's mind raced back and forth, pulling him between an intense desire to beat the living hell out of Wilks and his need to finish the job, get his money, and be free from Tanner Greene. *Fuck! How do I keep getting myself into these messes?* Mike turned to Vince and Franco, who sat quietly in the back.

"Who's fuckin' side are you two on?"

Vince looked shocked, "Whadaya mean, Mike? We work for you."

"No. You work for Mr. Greene. What I'm gettin' at is this, JC doesn't know what the fuck he's doin'. He's a god damned diva who's gonna get us busted if he keeps tryin' to make this about more than just gettin' rid of Younger. So, if it comes down to doin' this thing his way or my way, where do your loyalties lay?"

Franco hung his head, "Look, Mike. We both got families. Getting on Greene's bad side wouldn't be good for us."

"Yeah," Vince added. "It seems like Mr. Greene wants this JC guy to handle things as he sees fit. Like, tryin' him out to be part of the team, ya know what I mean? We're just here to help him get that done. We're all on the same side here, boss."

Mike turned back around. He knew Tanner had dirt on Vince and Franco but didn't know the full extent of it. Neither man could be trusted if Mike decided to go against JC. So, his only option now was to bide his time and see how JC's plan proceeded. Hopefully, he wouldn't get them all killed.

Chapter 21

The meeting with Mike and JC left Case feeling tense and unsettled. He paced the living room floor like a caged animal, acutely aware of how his restlessness was affecting his mood. He needed to do something productive before it turned to anger, so he grabbed his range gear and headed toward the barn.

It only took him an hour or so, but once he was finished, Case stood back and admired his handiwork. On a flat piece of ground just below the hillside adjacent to the barn, he'd planted three treated 4x4 posts in the ground, six feet apart, then screwed two more posts horizontally between each of the two sections, giving him four separate platforms where he could sit targets. Once that was finished, Case rummaged through the dark recesses of the barn and came away with an old feed sack full of empty oil cans, coke bottles, and plastic containers. He carried the load to his makeshift target stand and lined the empty bottles and cans up, equally spaced, along the rails, then paced out ten yards and kicked a line in the dirt at his feet. After that, Case emptied the expensive Hornady ammo he kept loaded in his Gen 5 Glock 19 and replaced it with standard ball ammunition. He reached into his range bag to retrieve his protective gear and stood to find Sam leaning against the edge of the barn. She wore a pair of Wiley-X wrap-around shooting glasses, Walker's noise-canceling EarPro, and her new Sig P365 XMACRO Comp.

"You didn't think you were gonna sneak out here and get some practice in on me, did you?"

Case smiled and swept an outstretched arm toward his line in the dirt, "Oh, by all means. Let's see what Bobby's taught ya since I've been gone."

Sam's face took on a more determined expression, "What are we shooting?"

"Here's what we'll do. There are eight total targets on the left and eight on the right. On my signal, we'll both draw from the holster and shoot till all eight of our targets are on the ground. But…" He added as Sam drew her pistol and performed an impressively smooth press check, "You have to perform a reload between the top and bottom rows. You good with that?"

Sam took her position on the line and twisted her feet in the dirt as if anchoring herself to the ground, "You call it."

Case looked over at Sam and nodded. Her stance was solid—feet shoulder-width apart, back straight, hands up above her waist in what street cops called an interview stance—non-threatening but ready. Case was impressed.

"Okay, we go on the command of 'up,'…shooters ready… up!"

Case didn't go for his pistol but instead took half a step back and turned to watch Sam. She was focused. Her posture had shifted into an aggressive shooting stance, with her shoulders forward and her hips back. Her movements were fluid. Her left hand remained in the centerline of her body while her right swept for the pistol. Once out of the holster, her hands met at chest level, wrapping the Sig in a perfect, thumbs-forward, two-handed grip. Case could see the readiness in her expression as she pressed the pistol forward and began a slow, steady press on the trigger. By the time she was at full extension, the weapon had fired.

The first round hit low. Wood splintered around the old

soda can, but it didn't fall. Sam followed up immediately with a second shot that hit, sending her target flying into the field. After that, she found her rhythm as target after target fell to the ground. Once the top row was destroyed, Sam performed a slow but methodical magazine exchange and returned to work on the second row of targets. Of the eight targets available, she'd only missed two but immediately followed up until she hit. Once the final can fell, Sam came back to a high-ready position and turned her head left and right to check her surroundings. It wasn't until her eyes came across Case that she realized he'd never even taken his gun out of the holster.

"What the hell, man? I thought this was a competition."

Case smiled and shook his head. "I just wanted to see how well you'd perform under pressure."

"And?" Sam asked.

"I gotta tell ya, Sam. I'm impressed to hell. Bobby did a good job teaching you, but there's a few things we still need to work on. The shots you missed were the first out of the holster and again after the reload; both were low, so there may be a problem with recoil anticipation. Tell ya what, I'll go set the targets back up. You top your magazines off, and we'll run a couple of drills to fix that."

Sam smiled. "Okay, but be careful what you teach me. I catch on quick, and I wouldn't want to embarrass a former federal air marshal on his own gun range."

Case laughed and winked at Sam, "That's why we're doing this behind the barn where no one can see."

Once back at the house, Case and Sam cleaned their pistols and stowed their range equipment. Case had shot a few rounds on his own, which impressed Sam, but he hadn't pushed himself the way he'd intended. He'd served as a firearms instructor long enough to know that when working with students of the craft, it was better to show them what *they* were capable of instead of what *you* were capable of, something a lot of newer instructors just didn't get. Case watched as Sam prepped her magazines with Gold Dot hollow points and reloaded her pistol before securing it in the safe next to Case's. She turned to find Case staring at her.

"What," She asked self-consciously.

"Nothing," Case responded, "I'm just proud of you, is all."

"For what?"

"It's just that a lot has changed since I came back, and most of its made life harder for you. And then I left again leaving you to deal with it on your own. I'm sorry for that."

Sam walked up to Case and placed the palms of her hands against his cheeks, forcing his eyes to hers. "Case, you're the reason Mia and I made it out of that mess last year alive. You're the reason that little girl up north made it back home, and you're the reason people here in Pikesville can breathe a little easier now. I know you feel like you broke some things, but that's not how it is. You did what was right."

Sam could feel Case's cheeks redden beneath her palms and knew she'd embarrassed him. She kissed him gently on the lips and dropped her hands.

"Now, since you put all that work in with me, how about you go find Mia, and I'll make us some supper, sound good?"

Case grabbed Sams hand as she started to turn away. "Sam, wait. I know I probably don't say this enough, but I think you and Mia are absolutely incredible—the way you've both handled yourselves lately—how you've managed to turn this rundown old house into a home even after everything that's happened. I just want you to know that I'm here now, and I understand the kind of thing you've both been through. It's tough, but you're not alone anymore. Okay?"

Case could see a little shiver course through Sam's body, so he pulled her in close without saying anything else. He waited until he felt her relax again before he let her go. Sam put her palms back on Case's face and kissed him one more time.

Twenty years. It had been twenty years since Case had initially left Pikesville. Looking at Sam now, he couldn't even remember the angry kid he'd been when he walked away; he just hoped that that piece of him would stay gone forever.

Part Two

Detonation

Chapter 22

Sam stood at the bar she'd inherited from her uncle, cleaning dirty glasses, as her backup bartender, Crystal, browsed the pages of *Bride Magazine*, researching centerpieces for Amanda's wedding reception. She had no idea so much work went into planning such a thing, but was more than willing to pitch in.

"Will the tables be circular or rectangular?" Crystal asked.

"That's a good question. I don't think Amanda mentioned it, but we can ask her tonight at the fitting."

"Well, it makes all the difference in the world when it comes to the centerpiece," Crystal said as she flipped the page.

"What? You read one bridal magazine, and suddenly, you're an expert on centerpieces." Sam teased.

Crystal rolled her eyes and returned to her article.

Business was usually slow between lunch and the evening regulars, so Sam was surprised when someone walked through the door so early in the afternoon. It was the young woman she'd seen at the baseball game with the guys from Maryland. She wore another pretty sundress. This one was light blue with small yellow flowers that hung elegantly from the girl's skinny frame.

"Hello there," Sam said from behind the bar. "You're the girl I saw at the game the other night with the Maryland scouts, right?"

"Yes, ma'am."

"Oh please, honey, call me Sam. Come on in and have a seat. This is Crystal."

Prissy smiled and sat at the bar beside Crystal, then straightened her dress with an unsteady hand. "It's nice to meet you. My name's Priscilla, but everyone just calls me Prissy."

"Can I get you a drink, Prissy?" Sam asked.

Prissy's eyes drifted longingly across the mirrored wall behind the bar, but her hesitation told Sam everything she needed to know. She'd been bartending long enough to recognize a recovering addict when she saw one, so she threw the girl a lifeline. "I have some bottled Cokes behind the bar if that sounds better. They're the good ones—with real sugar."

"I'd like that. Thank you," Prissy said as she started to relax.

Sam reached into the cooler, opened a frosty bottle, and sat it on the bar in front of Prissy. "So, how long will you guys be in town?"

"I'm not sure. They don't tell me anything. A couple of weeks, I guess."

"Where are you guys staying?"

"At the Motor Lodge just down the street. I just got tired of hanging out with the men and wanted to explore a bit."

"Sweetie, you've come to the right place. Just us girls in here for now."

"You don't even know what a welcome change that is," Prissy said.

Prissy had grown up in Goodman, Mississippi, a small town much like Pikesville, where the median income was barely enough to keep food on the table. Her father had worked in a lumber mill, and her mother found employment at an assisted living facility on the outskirts of Holmes County. But that only lasted until she got caught stealing pain medication. Prissy's father didn't hang around long after that. He took off six months later, leaving Prissy to care for her mom alone. The financial burden that created forced Prissy to drop out of high school and take a job as a gas station attendant. The plan was to scrape together enough money to leave Mississippi for good, but once she started getting high with Scott, the manager, it didn't take long to realize she'd never have enough. So, on her seventeenth birthday, Prissy used her meager savings to buy a quarter bag of weed and a bus ticket to carry her as far away from Goodman as possible. She made it as far as Richmond, Virginia.

At first, she'd found work waiting tables at a local diner, but the pay was barely enough to keep a roof over her head. That's when she met Tucker. He was a lot older than Prissy and not exactly the type of man she'd typically be attracted to, but he was a regular customer and tipped well—so well, in fact, that it covered her monthly rent, which, as it turns out, was Tucker's plan all along. When he finally asked her out, Prissy felt obligated to say yes.

One night, shortly after she and Tucker started dating, Prissy woke up to people screaming and fighting in the hallway. Then, the sound of sirens and motorcycles roaring away in the distance. The commotion scared Prissy, so she stayed locked behind the flimsy door of her apartment until it was light out. When she ran into her landlord, Mr. Kapoor, the next morning, he handed her an eviction notice and walked away without an explanation. He'd given her one week. Then she'd be back on the street. That's when Tucker stepped in to save the day. He offered to let Prissy crash at the house he and his friends used as a party pad. There were other girls there, and drugs, lots of drugs. Before long, Prissy was hooked. She never went back to the diner. She didn't need to. The club afforded her the essentials—food, shelter, and a constant high in exchange for the use of her body. At first, she was appalled and refused, but after a good beating from Tucker, she decided it was in her best interest to do as she was told. With her mind twisted by meth and heroin, Prissy lost sight of who she was and, over the years, resigned herself to life as a prostitute. After her time in jail, JC helped clean her up and got her down from the drugs. But now, with a clear mind, she found herself in an even bigger mess and struggled with the morality of it all.

"So that man at the game, the one who talked to JC and Mike, are y'all gettin' married?" Prissy asked, pointing at the bridal magazine in Crystal's hand.

"Case? No. The wedding is for his brother, Bobby, and his fiancé Amanda."

"I've always loved weddings," Prissy said. "The idea of them anyway."

"Case told me you were engaged to one of the scouts," Sam said quizzically.

Prissy realized her mistake. "Yeah, JC and I are engaged, but we haven't set a date or started planning anything yet."

Crystal piped up from her perch on the barstool, "Oh my God, you should totally come with us tonight. We're picking Amanda up later for the final fitting of her dress. Maybe you could get some ideas for yours."

Prissy didn't know how to respond. JC had told her to get close to Sam, but it was all happening so fast. Everyone was so nice and trusting, she felt horrible for taking advantage of that.

"I wouldn't want to impose."

"Nonsense," Sam said. "It'll be fun. Besides, it'll get you out of that motel and away from the men for a while. You should come."

Prissy hesitated, but the thought of time away from JC made her smile. "Okay. That sounds great."

The three women chatted and laughed as Prissy finished her Coke. Before leaving, Sam and Crystal agreed to pick her up from the motel at six. When Prissy walked out of the bar, she felt happier than she had in years, but suddenly, the realization of what she was about to do sank in, and Prissy started to hate herself again.

Chapter 23

Case walked in from the barn to find Sam setting food on the table. She worked late most nights, so Case usually made supper for Mia, which meant either frozen pizzas or TV dinners—the extent of Case's culinary talents. When she was home, Sam always made it a point to serve a decent meal to make up for the nights she was away. She rushed from the kitchen to the dining room, laying out big porcelain bowls of bone-in pork chops, potatoes, rolls, and green beans. Case's favorite.

"What's this? Are we eating early tonight?" He asked, kissing Sam on the cheek as he stepped to the sink and washed his hands.

"Yeah, sorry it's so early. I wanted to leave by 5:30 tonight to get Crystal. We're going to Amanda's final dress fitting." Sam explained before yelling down the hall, "Mia! Get in here. It's time for supper."

"Wow. That's coming up quick."

"Yeah. We have the final dress fitting tonight and then the rehearsal dinner next Saturday. Oh, and I invited that girl along from the ball game the other night. The one who was there with the scouts."

"Really?" Case asked as Mia sat beside him, enthusiastically digging into a big bowl of mashed potatoes—obviously happy to see a meal that hadn't come from a cardboard box.

"Yeah. She came into the bar this afternoon and sat for a while. She seemed really sweet but kinda sad. I guess they'll be here for a week or two, so Crystal and I thought it would be nice to get to know her. Plus, maybe it'll help Trevor if she puts a good word in for us."

Case hadn't said much about his encounter with JC at the game but decided it was time to fill Sam in on Dimpsey's misgivings about the man.

"The other day, the scout came into the hardware store and spoke to Dimpsey and Trevor. Dimpsey feels a little uneasy about the guy."

"And what about you?" Sam asked.

"I don't know. The guy seemed a little standoffish when I spoke to him, but I'm sure he needs to be—getting approached like that at games all the time. His partner, Mike, seemed nice enough though. Me, Dimpsey, and Trevor are meeting them for breakfast in the morning."

"Trevor's so excited," Mia said between forks full of food.

"Trevor's always excited." Case replied as he thought back to his encounter with JC. The awkwardness of it still circulating in his mind. "Sam, do me a favor. Tonight, when you're with the girl would you get as much information as you can about her fiancé, JC—when they met, how, where, who their friends are."

"Okay. Any particular reason for all the personal questions?"

Case didn't want to say anything further in front of Mia, so he played it off. "It's just small talk, so I can learn a little about who we're dealing with before breakfast tomorrow."

Sam knew Case wasn't being completely open but didn't press the issue. "Sure. We can talk tonight when I get back."

JC paced back and forth across the worn-out carpet of the motel room as Mike sat on the edge of the bed, watching Prissy pick a dress for her night out. Vince and Franco sat at the small table by the window playing cards.

"Listen to me, Prissy. We have an opportunity here, so don't fuck this up."

Prissy huffed. "I won't, JC. You told me to get close to Case's girlfriend, and I did."

"And what are you going to do for me tonight?"

Prissy struggled to recall JC's instructions. She was much more concerned about looking presentable and making a good impression on her new friends.

"What the fuck, Prissy. We just went over this!" JC yelled.

"Give the girl a break, Wilks," Mike said from the edge of the bed. "She's doin' everything you told her to. Just give her a second to think about it."

"Did I ask your opinion on this, Mike?"

Mike shrugged and turned his attention back to Prissy, who held up another dress. "That one's nice, Ms. Priscilla. You should wear that one."

Priscilla smiled at Mike and set the dress aside.

"You're gonna cozy up to these women and get the two of us invited to that wedding." JC continued. "That puts us in the same room with everyone on my list. Then, you'll get as much detail as you can about what's happening, where it'll be, how many people will be attending, who, everything you can. The groom's a fucking cop, so definitely find out how many of his friends will be there."

"I'll do my best, JC, I promise."

"No, Prissy. You're going to get this done. Do you understand me?"

Prissy hung her head. "I understand, JC."

"Good, Me and Prince Charming here," JC said, pointing to Mike, "will talk to Case and the old man at breakfast in the morning. If this all goes well, we'll all be one big happy family by the time this wedding rolls around."

JC walked into the other room, leaving the others alone. He didn't know how much longer he could put up with Mike's lip or Prissy's inability to stay on task. Apparently, she was far more interested in palling around with the girls than getting Case out of the picture. Despite his selfish nature, JC missed the single-minded efficiency of the club—everyone working together. He missed the camaraderie. Outside of the club, he'd never been one to work well with others. After graduating from business school, his father wanted him to pursue a career in corporate law, but he had other plans. He knew the trust fund money would keep him in the lifestyle he was accustomed to, so why not do something different, something exciting, if it pissed his dad off in the process, all the better. That's when he met Lucky.

JC had always been somewhat of a thrill seeker. Whether it was women, drugs, bikes, or breaking the law, he was all in. One night, he'd hooked up with a girl who said she could take him somewhere he'd never been and introduce him to some people who could provide him with all the excitement he wanted. Not one to back down from the promise of a good time, JC soon found himself at the Rusty Spoke, surrounded by men in jean vests who looked as if they didn't give two fucks about how the world viewed them. They drank, smoked, and openly discussed their plans for expanding their business into prostitution and trafficking. It hooked JC immediately, and he knew he needed to be a part of it. At first, the club shunned JC as an outsider, but once he proved his value by breaking down the business end of the trafficking operation to Lucky and a guy named Rex, he was brought in as an official prospect and mentored by Lucky himself. After a year of being treated like a servant to the club, running errands, washing bikes, and keeping the girls in line, he earned his patch and was made an official part of the Dead Rebels Richmond chapter. He only took a year to maximize the club's profits and line their pockets with enough cash to keep the cops off their backs and everyone happy. After that, he was made the club's official Sergeant at Arms and got a vote at the officer's table. That's when he introduced the club to Tanner Greene and the promise of a lucrative future in the trafficking business. There was no way he would let a two-bit hood like Mike and some whore ruin that for him. He'd end them both if it meant getting even with Case and securing his position within Stonehill. It was all that mattered and he'd stop at nothing to make it happen.

Chapter 24

Sam pulled up at Country Formals Bridal Shop with Amanda, Crystal, and Prissy. They parked on Main Street and walked the length of town so they could point out some of the more prominent local sites to Prissy before circling back to the dress shop. It only took a few minutes before they were standing back at the entrance.

"So, that's the big city of Pikesville, huh?" Prissy asked jokingly.

"It's very cosmopolitan, isn't it?" Crystal quipped in return.

"I think it's lovely. I could see myself settling down in a place like this one day."

"You think JC would go for that?"

Prissy kept forgetting that she was supposed to be engaged.

"Who knows? Maybe one day. But today is about the bride-to-be, so let's get in here and see this amazing dress I keep hearing about."

They all talked excitedly as they were greeted at the door by Michelle, the owner, who offered them tall plastic flutes of champagne to celebrate the occasion. Sam saw the look on Prissy's face and interceded.

"Oh, none for me, thanks. I'm drivin'."

Prissy followed suit. "I believe I'll pass too, thank you." After the past few weeks sober, she felt better than she had in years and didn't want to ruin it.

Sam leaned over and whispered in Prissy's ear. "Champagne gives me a headache anyway. Who needs that, right?"

"Yeah. Who needs it?" Prissy replied gratefully.

Amanda stood on a short wooden pedestal as Michelle and Crystal walked around the dress, discussing last-minute alterations. Sam and Prissy sat together in the corner on a plush white sofa, chatting casually about growing up in a small town.

"So, tell me about JC. How did you two meet?" Sam asked, steering the conversation in the direction Case had asked her to.

JC hadn't told her what to say if the topic of their relationship came up, so the question threw her off.

"Um, we met at a fundraiser in Richmond."

The answer was vague, so Sam pressed a little further. "Really? What was the fundraiser for?"

"I'm not sure. I was just waiting tables." Prissy offered hurriedly before turning her attention back to the dress.

"How long have you guys been together?"

"Two years," She said.

Sam liked Prissy. She was sweet and shy, but Sam could tell her line of questioning was making the girl uncomfortable. After a few minutes of silence between the two, Sam changed the subject.

"Ya know, If you guys will be in town for a while longer, you should come to the wedding."

Prissy sat up and looked genuinely excited for a moment, but the happiness in her eyes faded quickly and was replaced by a sadness Sam didn't quite understand.

"I don't mean to overstep, Prissy. If you're not comfortable—"

"No. I'd love to come. It's just…"

"What?" Sam asked.

"I don't know. I can ask JC. But I wouldn't want to impose

on Amanda's big day."

Sam placed a hand on Prissy's knee. "Look, this isn't gonna be anything big. It's just family and a few close friends. Nothing crazy. I know Amanda won't mind, and I'm sure Trevor would love seeing JC there. Just talk to him about it, okay? It'll be fun, and besides, you just saw the entire town of Pikesville in less than five minutes, what else is there to do around here?"

Amanda overheard the conversation from her perch on the pedestal and agreed, "Come on Priscilla. We'd love to have you there. You and JC are more than welcome to join us."

"Okay," Prissy said with a hollow smile, trying to feign happiness at the invitation. "I'll see what JC thinks about it."

That evening back at the motel, Prissy didn't have much to say. Her mind felt twisted by what she was doing. JC was ecstatic that she'd landed an invitation to the wedding so easily, but she had a hard time pretending to be on board with the plan. Prissy liked Sam. The time they'd spent together had shown her an entirely different world outside the one she was living in—one filled with kindness and friendship. But those feelings only made what she had to do more painful. She knew her sobriety also played a role in how she was feeling. The longer Prissy stayed sober, the more she remembered the type of person she was before meeting Tucker, and that person wouldn't treat a friend the way she was treating Sam. Prissy had never been perfect, but she'd certainly never been an accessory to anything like this. The contradictions swirling in her mind felt like they would tear her apart.

"You did good, Prissy. This is really good."

"Thanks, JC."

JC could tell there was something else on the girl's mind, "What's wrong?"

Mike sat by the window, watching Prissy struggle with what to say. "She's obviously uncomfortable with this plan of yours, JC."

JC turned his attention to Mike, "Oh, is that right? I guess we'll just scrap the whole thing then because, God forbid, this one develops a fucking conscience and gets sad about doing her goddamn job!" JC yelled as he turned back to Prissy.

Prissy cowered on the bed as JC hovered over her. Mike stayed calm despite his yearning to grab JC by the throat and beat the life out of him. "That's unnecessary, JC."

"Oh, that's unnecessary? Well, let me tell you what *is* necessary, Mike. It's necessary that this man pay for what he did. Tanner Greene wants Case dead for destroying his lucrative little side venture, but I want more than that now. I want that son-of-a-bitch to suffer the same kind of loss my club did. That man burned five of my brothers alive, then just drove away like it never happened. So, now we're going to do the same thing to him."

Mike looked at JC without malice or emotion, but found the sudden change of plan concerning. "Okay then, why don't you fill us in on this new and improved plan of yours."

Vince, Franco and Prissy all stared at JC waiting for him to continue.

"We have one week till the wedding. We know it'll be outdoors, but the reception will be in the golf course's banquet hall. From what Prissy told us, it's going to be a small event with just a few friends and family. Once everyone is inside, Prissy and I will slip out the back, then you, Vince, and Franco will chain the door and torch the place. If anyone makes it out, we pick them off from the parking lot. Like shooting fish in a barrel."

Mike tried to appeal to JC's logical side. "There's a lot of moving parts there, JC. And there's gonna to be a lot of people there who weren't involved in any of this, cooks, wait staff—kids. Don't you think it would be easier just to catch Case alone and take him out quietly? That'll satisfy Mr. Greene, you'll have what you want, and we lessen the risk of gettin' caught—or worse."

JC didn't like being questioned. His father used to do that to him—pick apart every decision he ever made. No way he was going to let some two-bit thug like Mike do the same thing. He was in charge now and no one was going to tell him how to handle his business.

"No. We do this my way. And just so we're clear, I don't give a shit how many of these white trash hillbillies get hurt. Now get the fuck away from me because quite frankly, Mike, you're—what's the word you used a minute ago—unnecessary."

Mike stood and looked to Vince and Franco, who both turned away. That told him everything he needed to know about who's side they were on. They'd back JC to cover their own asses with Tanner. Mike nodded and walked to the door without saying anything else. Before leaving, he glanced back at Prissy, who sat on the edge of the bed, looking back at him. Mike winked and closed the door between them.

In all the commotion, Prissy forgot to tell JC about the questions Sam had asked her at the bridal shop—simple questions that they should have prepared for but didn't. By the time Prissy remembered it was getting late and JC was in no mood for conversation. She wasn't about to risk upsetting him over something so trivial. *It'll be fine*, she thought before slipping into bed. *Men never talk about things like that, anyway.*

Chapter 25

The next morning, Mike woke up with a lot on his mind. Mr. Greene paid well, and the money put him one step closer to walking away from his past and starting over somewhere new, but he could see the pain this was causing Prissy and didn't like watching the girl struggle. Mike knew they both questioned JC's scheme. He just needed to get her alone to talk to her—to tell her that he understood.

Mike placed his feet on the well-worn '70s-style carpet and walked to the shower. Vince tossed restlessly on the couch while Franco slept in the bed across from Mike's. *This is gettin' stupid,* he told himself as he stripped down and waited for the water to heat up. He didn't know what Tanner had on his crew, but they were obviously going along with whatever JC said simply because they felt that's what Tanner wanted. That left him and Prissy on the outside. If something went sideways with JC's plan, which was very likely, they'd be the expendable ones. Over the years, he'd done a lot of things he wasn't proud of, but this was different. JC was so hellbent on revenge and ingratiating himself with Greene, that it clouded his judgement. His willingness to kill innocents just to prove a point put them all at risk, and that was something Mike couldn't allow. He needed a plan of his own.

Mike always thought more clearly when his body was stressed, so he stepped into the steaming shower and pulled the cheap plastic curtain closed behind him. Tiny beads of scalding water pelted his skin until it burned bright red. He breathed deeply—in and out, absorbing the discomfort until he felt himself relax. Then he took one last breath and held it before turning the knob all the way over to cold. The shock instantly forced his body into survival mode. Mike tried to control his breathing as his body fought to adapt—just like in BUD/s. After what felt like an eternity, his heart rate stabilized and he exhaled slowly, focusing all of his thoughts on one problem—the best way to get him and Prissy out of this mess alive.

Case walked into the diner with Dimpsey and Trevor, who greeted Peggy, their waitress.

"Hey, Peggy. We have a super important meeting this morning with some baseball scouts, so can you sit us someplace quiet." Trevor asked.

Peggy smiled, "Well, of course I can, mister bigshot. Follow me."

Dimpsey looked at Case and shook his head. "These guys better not be jerking us around. It'll break that boy's heart."

Peggy walked them into the back dining area and sat them at their most private table in the corner, away from the kitchen. Case took a seat facing the entrance.

"Trevor, do me a favor, buddy. Could you run back up front and ask Peggy for some hot sauce, please?"

"Sure thing," Trevor said as he stood and returned to the counter.

Case turned to Dimpsey. "That'll buy us a minute. I spoke to Sam about these guys. She actually met up with Prissy yesterday, JC's fiancé. The girl stopped by the bar and Sam was able to get some personal information about how her and JC met."

"Okay, what do we do with that?" Dimpsey asked.

"While we're talking baseball this morning, I figured I could slip in a few personal questions to see if their stories line up."

"So, you think this feels off too?"

"I do. But it needs to be confirmed and I didn't want to say anything in front of Trevor. You're right. It'll break his heart if they're not who they say they are."

"What would they be doing in Pikesville otherwise?"

"I don't know, but I think it's best to play it safe and learn as much about these guys as we can for now. We'll figure out what to do with the information later."

"Sounds good to me. I'll follow your lead." Dimpsey responded.

As a Federal Air Marshal, Case had gotten pretty good at bullshitting people. While most folks boarded the plane lost in their own little world, never looking at or speaking to the people around them, inevitably, he'd get stuck sitting next to someone who couldn't stop asking questions. In those cases, he needed to be polite and conversational while still maintaining his vigilance and keeping an eye out for threats. That required him to memorize a cover story explaining who he was, where he was going, and what he would do when he landed. In the beginning, Case had a foolproof yarn about being a procurement specialist for a chemical company—something so mundane and boring that no one dared ask follow-up questions about it. But as time passed, he'd learned to have a little more fun with it. Making up tall tales on the fly and drawing people into his fictional life became a fun way to kill time on those long international flights. His favorite became convincing people that he was a pigeon farmer from Las Vegas—collecting a special breed of white homing pigeons that could be rented out and released at weddings only to return to him, then rented out over and over again. The more Case told the story, the more he convinced himself that it could be a lucrative source of income. He would even jokingly tell coworkers he was considering it as a profession once he retired. It was always fun to watch their reactions.

One beneficial side effect of his ability to deceive people was that he'd also learned to pick up on other people's lies. A skill that he intended to apply to this morning's conversation with the scouts. Just then, Trevor returned to the table carrying a bottle of hot sauce, followed closely by JC and Mike.

"Look who I found," Trevor said excitedly.

Case and Dimpsey stood and shook hands with the men before sitting back down and picking up their menus. Everyone was cordial and polite, but there was a seriousness about JC that seems out of place for such a casual gathering.

As they talked, it became apparent to Case that Mike was the only one who knew anything at all about baseball. While Peggy loaded the table with plates of scrambled eggs, salted ham, biscuits, and gravy, he spoke excitedly about his beloved Yankees. They hadn't won a World Series since 2009, but he remained hopeful for a playoff championship this year.

After breakfast, their conversation turned to their military service and the places they'd been. Again, JC didn't have much to say, but Case and Mike concluded that their paths had probably crossed several times during the global war on terror. Case enjoyed Mike's company but needed to turn the conversation back to JC.

"So, how long have you been with Maryland, JC?"

JC cleaned the corners of his mouth with a paper napkin

before answering. "I guess it's been three or four years now. You know how it goes. At a certain point everything just starts to blend together and you lose track."

"I suppose being a scout does keep you busy," Dimpsey added.

JC nodded, "Yes, it does."

"So, Sam tells me she's been spending time with your fiancé, Priscilla. I hear you guys will be coming to the wedding."

This was news to Dimpsey, who tried to mask his displeasure by taking a long pull from his coffee.

"I suppose so. I hope that's no imposition. Prissy tends to overstep sometimes."

"It's no problem at all. Sam likes her a lot. It would be nice if you could come too, Mike." Case said, looking over at his new friend.

Mike smiled, "Sure. It would be an honor."

Case turned his attention back to JC, who was now staring at Mike. "How long have the two of you been engaged?"

Shit! JC was caught off guard. They hadn't thought to cover this in their planning, so he started improvising again. "We just met a few months ago. It's been one of those whirlwind romances, I guess you could say."

"Where did you meet?" Case asked.

JC shifted uncomfortably in his chair wondering what Prissy had discussed with Sam. "Oh. She was a former student. We ran into each other one night at a bar, and things took off from there."

"I see." Case said, staring back across the table at JC. *This is all off. Something's not right.*

The conversation continued, but every time Case would bring up something personal, JC would deflect and change the subject—a sure sign he was being purposefully dishonest. It was of no consequence though; Case already knew JC wasn't who he said he was. The only thing he could do now was keep an eye on the man until he knew why him and his crew had come to Pikesville.

After Peggy cleared the table, Case picked up the tab, and everyone said their goodbyes. JC promised Trevor that he'd keep an eye on him and put him on the list of future recruits, but nothing could happen until after he graduated, and only if his grades were good enough. That was all Trevor needed to hear. The boy seemed ready to jump out of his skin by the time they all parted ways. Case and Dimpsey remained silent as they drove back to the farm. Both men knew they had a lot to discuss once they were clear of Trevor.

Chapter 26

Once back at the farm, it didn't take long for Trevor and Mia to disappear together, leaving Case, Dimpsey, and Sam alone to discuss their concerns about the so-called scouts.

"So, what did you guys find out?" Sam asked as she poured two cups of coffee and carried them to the table for Case and Dimpsey.

"We found out that this Wilks guy is full of shit, that's what," Dimpsey responded.

"Really?" Sam asked, now looking to Case.

"Yeah. Nothing adds up. Nothing Priscilla told you about how they met matches what he told me. He barely had two words to say about baseball. The guy obviously isn't who he says he is."

"What about the other one?"

"Mike. Mike's hard to read. He seems genuine, and he's a likable guy. But if he's with JC, he can't be trusted. Neither can Prissy."

"So, what do we do? Hell, we invited them to Bobby and Amanda's wedding, Case."

"Not a good idea." Dimpsey said shaking his head.

"Nothing we can do about that now. I'll talk to Bobby and we'll dig a little deeper into this. In the meantime, stay close to Prissy. Dimpsey, you can put your ear to the ground at the hardware store and see if anyone else around here has spoken with these guys or if all their attention is focused solely on us."

"Will do," Dimpsey said between sips of coffee.

Case couldn't help but admire the man. His strength and quiet calm had always served to put Case's mind at ease during hard times, and now was no different.

Sam, however, looked concerned. "Case, should we be worried about any of this? I mean, with everything that's happened in the past year—could this be tied to any of that somehow?"

"I'm not sure, but I will find out."

Bobby had finally made the move into Sunny's old office and stared absentmindedly at the phone, sitting amidst the clutter of his new desk. After Case filled him in on what was happening, they both thought it would be best to approach this from a professional angle, so Case had Bobby put in an official call to the University of Maryland. After several minutes of waiting, a woman's voice came back over the speaker.

"I'm sorry for the wait, sheriff. I've searched everything here, and we have no record of anyone with the last name Wilks or Moretti working in our athletics department."

"Okay, and you're sure they don't use outside employees for scouting or recruiting efforts?"

"I'm certain of it, sir. We do all that in-house. We always have."

"I appreciate you looking into this for me, ma'am. You've been a tremendous help."

Bobby hung-up and looked across his desk at Case.

"What the hell, Case? Who are these men, and why are they sniffing around Pikesville posing as baseball scouts?"

"That's what I'm trying to find out."

"Does this have anything to do with what happened in Grandview?" Bobby asked.

When Case first returned to Pikesville, the problems with Jesse Williams and the bikers squatting in Grandview trailer park accelerated into a literal inferno. When Bobby stopped at the farm that night to check in on his brother, he was caught in an ambush set by Jesse to kill Case and was shot twice. Bobby knew he wouldn't be alive today if Case hadn't found him lying on the living room floor. They both hoped this wasn't an extension of what happened that night.

"I don't know." Case responded. "I've picked this apart as best I can and can't find a connection to Jesse, Rex, or any of the guys involved with Grandview. Maybe you could reach out to Detective Wayne and see what he can find."

"I can do that, but Sam invited them to the wedding, didn't she?"

"She did, but I wish she hadn't. She wasn't aware of our suspicions at the time."

"No. I think it's best this way. Keep your friends close and your enemies closer, right?"

Case smiled as he stood to leave, "You've been reading Sun Tzu?"

"Who's that?" Bobby said, trying to lighten the mood. "We'll figure this out. In the meantime, let me see what Dillon can come up with. You and Dimpsey just keep your eyes and ears open. If these guys step out of line, I want to be the first to know about it, okay? No more cowboy shit."

Case stopped at the door. "Why does everyone keep saying that?"

Bobby shook his head and waited for Case to leave before picking the phone up again.

"Hey, Bonnie, could you patch me through to Detective Dillon Wayne with the state police, please."

Chapter 27

JC paced back and forth in the tiny motel room, waiting for Celia to put him through to Tanner Greene. Despite Mike's doubts, he felt like everything was coming together nicely in Pikesville and hoped Greene would be pleased with his updated plan. He didn't really care about Greene. It wasn't like he'd ever given a shit about what other people thought, but with Tanner, JC saw an opportunity. As an asset to Stonehill, he could have the lavish lifestyle he was accustomed to and still be involved with the more nefarious aspects of the criminal world. The perfect balance. His brothers in the club may have been happy with the scraps Greene threw them from time to time, but JC wasn't about to settle. He wanted more. He wanted a seat at the big table, and taking care of the Pikesville situation for Tanner was his way in.

After several minutes, Tanner's voice came over the line. "This is Greene."

"Mr. Greene, it's JC."

"I'm aware, Mr. Wilks. What do you have for me?"

"I just wanted to let you know this Pikesville thing will all be over soon. I have a lock on Younger."

There was an exaggerated pause before Tanner responded, "Michael tells me you've concocted some elaborate scheme to eliminate more than just Mr. Younger."

JC felt his face flood with anger. "Sir, it's a good plan and when it's done, no one within a hundred miles of this place will ever interfere with you or your business again. I can promise you that. Moretti shouldn't have gone behind my back."

"Mr. Wilks, Michael, works for *me*. He reports to *me,* and he will do as *I* tell him. Is that clear to you?"

JC tried to calm himself. He didn't want to blow his only shot of making a good impression on Tanner, "Crystal, sir."

"Good. Now, let me spell this out for you. You and I are approaching this from very different angles. I'm looking at this from a purely business perspective. Mr. Younger is an obstacle to my future trade in that area, so I need him removed. You, on the other hand, are taking this assignment very personally."

"Mr. Greene, I—"

"Don't interrupt me, Mr. Wilks!" Greene hissed into the phone. "I'll allow you to carry on with your plot against Younger, but if I so much as hear a whisper that this is getting out of hand or that you are running the risk of exposing my business, neither you nor Mr. Younger will fare well in this endeavor. Do you understand me?"

"I understand, Mr. Greene."

"Very well."

The line went dead, and JC was left standing in the middle of the room, trembling with rage. *Who the fuck does this guy think he's dealing with?* JC closed his eyes and tried to calm himself. He could hear the faint sound of Prissy and Moretti laughing from the other side of the wall. Still fuming, he reached under the mattress of his bed and grabbed the pistol he'd hidden away. Someone needed to learn their fucking place.

Mike sat on the ragged motel couch watching TV with Prissy while Vince and Franco were out gathering the supplies they'd need to make Molotov cocktails—another unnecessary element in JC's newly concocted scheme. Sun spilled through the open windows and cast a glare over the small television screen, but Mike wasn't really paying attention to what was on. He was just enjoying his downtime with Prissy. She jumped when JC burst through the door, gun in hand.

Mike stood and placed himself between the gun and the girl, with his hands in the air. "Whoa, JC. What's happening here?"

"What's happening? You, Mike, you're what's happening." JC hissed, trembling with rage.

"If your beef is with me, then let's not involve her," Mike said, nodding his head toward Prissy.

"Fuck you! She stays."

"Okay, okay. I don't know what's going through your mind right now, but you're looking a little fuckin' shaky, so why don't you just put the gun down?"

JC raised the gun and pointed it at Mike, "Did you go behind my back and snitch to Greene?"

Mike stepped closer to JC. His eyes conveying everything he was feeling. JC took a step back.

"Tanner told me to check in with him daily. I'm just following orders. And up to this point, I've done everything you've asked me to do, whether I liked it or not. But if you don't put that gun down right now, I swear on my mother's grave, I'm gonna take it from you and beat you to death with it."

Mike saw the doubt in JC's eyes. He knew JC was a bully and bullies were often cowards. JC lowered the gun. Prissy pulled her feet onto the couch and hugged her knees, trying to make herself as small as possible.

"Good." Mike continued. "Now we can talk about this like men."

"You shouldn't have told Greene you had doubts about the plan."

"I get that you want this guy to pay for what he did to you, but your plan is gonna get one of us killed."

"The plan stands, Mike. You can bitch to Greene all you want, but we do this my way."

Mike kept his eyes locked on Wilks. "Whatever you say, JC. But know this. I won't hurt anybody innocent for a fuckin' guy like you. If you want everybody on that stupid list of yours dead, then you'll be doing that without me."

"You don't think I can?"

"I think you can hurt people, JC, but not people stronger than you. And I certainly don't think you can take me or a man like Case. So, you do what you have to, but don't ever come at me or Prissy like this again. Understood?"

JC stared at Mike, struggling to maintain some semblance of authority. "Prissy, get in the other room."

Prissy did as she was told, but Mike never broke eye contact with JC. "You hurt that girl, and I'll hurt you, JC."

JC backed away, smirking, then closed the door between them. Mike stood in the center of the room. He needed this paycheck to be out from under Tanner's thumb, but he also needed to figure out how to collect without getting himself or Prissy killed. JC would have to be dealt with.

Mike sat back down and turned toward the television, but his mind stayed focused on the current problem and the best way to escape the mess JC was creating.

Chapter 28

It was evening, and Case was exhausted. He and Sam had spent the rest of the day scraping and painting the front porch to spruce the place up and take his mind off the issue with Wilks and Moretti. He'd just sat down in his dad's old recliner when he heard a knock at the door.

"I got it," Sam said as she walked in from the hallway.

"Bobby. Come on in."

Bobby stepped inside and hugged Sam before sitting on the couch across from Case.

"Can I get you something to drink?" She asked.

"No thanks, Sam. I appreciate it though." Bobby waited for Sam to walk away before saying anything else.

"So, I called Dillon right after you left today."

Case sat up in his chair, "And?"

"Your man Wilks came back clean. He got into some trouble as a kid, but over the past fifteen years, he hasn't had so much as a speeding ticket."

"What about Moretti?"

"Moretti's a different story. Things started off good for him. It looks like he had his shit together. But he got caught stealing a considerable amount of cash during an op in Afghanistan. He was drummed out of the Navy and pulled five years in Leavenworth. Now, he works as head of security for a company called Stonehill Investment Group in New York, which is run by a man named Tanner Greene."

"Any connection between Greene and JC?"

"Nothing we could find."

"So, these guys aren't baseball scouts at all?" Sam said from the doorway.

Bobby was startled when he realized Sam hadn't left the room. He didn't want to upset her, but knew better than to be dishonest. "No, they're not. But they don't seem to be connected to what happened here last year either. Personally, I think it may be best just to confront these guys and see what they're after here in Pikesville."

Case considered the option. "I don't know, Bobby. I don't want these guys to think we suspect anything just yet. I don't want to scare them away, and if this is somehow connected to the Grandview operation, I need to know for sure."

"Okay," Bobby said. "We'll play this your way. But I need you to promise me something. If this starts looking like it could go sideways, you have to let me know. These people will be at my wedding, Case."

"I know Bobby, and I will. But if it's okay with you and Amanda, I have a couple more friends I'd like to invite to the wedding."

Matt Barrett stood in front of the conference room whiteboard, prioritizing the CMP's mission list, when his phone rang. Over the past few months, he'd worked his way up the chain to become Andre's number two and the leader of his own team. He was honored to have the position, but with it came more administrative work than he liked. The phone call offered him a reprieve. Matt looked down at the caller ID to see it was Case.

"Case. My man. What's up?"

"Hey, Matt. It's good to hear your voice. How's Ross and the rest of the team?"

"It's all good up here, brother. How are things with you?"

"Things are good here, but I could use a favor."

"Oh shit."

"Relax. I'm just calling to invite you and Ross to a wedding."

"That was quick."

Case laughed. "It's not mine. It's my brother Bobby's."

Matt was quiet for a few seconds. "Okay. And why would you need Ross and me at your little brother's wedding?"

"There're some guys in town who've managed to get close to my family and me, and they'll be attending. Now, it's come to light that they're not being honest about who they are and what they want."

"So, uninvite them."

"I wish it was that easy, buddy. These guys are here for a reason, and it somehow involves me. If this is connected to what happened last year, I'd rather keep them close. Plus, if I don't deal with this now it's bound to come back and I might not see it coming next time."

"I understand. When's the wedding?"

"It's this Sunday."

"Damn, Case. That's short notice. Let me run this past Brown and see what I can do."

"Fair enough. I appreciate it, Matt."

"You know, these favors are starting to add up."

"I know."

"I'll be in touch."

Matt hung up and yelled into the bullpen. "Ross! Get your suit cleaned. We're going to a wedding."

Chapter 29

Sam sat alone on the back porch, staring out into the distance. She could barely distinguish between the fading silhouettes of cows and calves as they grazed along the ridge behind the barn. It was a serene and peaceful sight, sharply contrasting with the feeling that something frightening lay just over the horizon, some unknown enemy that could storm the hillside at any moment and destroy everything. Things had changed since Case left the Air Marshal service and returned to Pikesville. Sure, it hadn't been easy with Jesse and Rex running around causing problems. But, even with them gone, Sam still felt uneasy. Life with Case had always been unpredictable; his temper seemed to be under control now, and he looked genuinely happy to be home, but with him, you never knew what might set him off. Things tended to get ugly when that happened, and she prayed this nonsense with the scouts wasn't one of those things. Finding out they weren't who they said they were troubled her, especially knowing that Prissy could be lying as well.

Sam remembered a conversation she'd had with her mother when she and Case first started dating. Pikesville was a tight-knit community, and most of the townspeople knew Case's mom, Molly Younger. She was a sweet woman, friendly and caring. When she passed away, there were rumblings around town that her husband, Avis, wouldn't be fit to raise two boys on his own—with his notoriously lousy temper and unpredictable moods, some considered him to be unstable. But Sam had seen another side of Avis and always came to his defense. She liked to believe what people showed her, not what they told her.

"I want you to watch yourself around that family, Sam. Those boys being raised without a mother…it's hard to tell how they might turn out."

"Mom. It's not like everyone says. Avis is good to me, and he's good to Case and Bobby. He just gets mad sometimes, but look at what he's been through. Uncle Bill is friends with him and he says Avis is still just a bit shell-shocked from the war is all."

Sam's mom huffed. "Just watch yourself is all I'm sayin'. The apple never falls too far from the tree, so if that boy starts acting crazy, I don't want you anywhere around him. You'd be better off finding yourself a good boy from church who lives in a stable home."

"Case isn't crazy, mom. They're all doin' the best they can, and I think me bein' around helps."

Back then, Sam didn't realize how right she'd been. Having her around did help. Her female presence brought a sense of civility to an otherwise chaotic home—something she intended to continue.

Sam stood and walked back inside. Despite his shortcomings, Case was the right man for her. She loved him deeply. She knew he loved her too and that her being in his life again helped to keep him grounded. He couldn't help what Rex and Jesse did, and he couldn't help how things turned out. It was comforting to know that side of Case existed—the side that would protect her and Mia no matter the cost. Sam made a vow to do the same. To be there for him, no matter what.

Mia stepped out of her bedroom just as Sam started down the hall.

"Hey, Mom. You okay?"

Sam was startled, "Yeah, baby, I'm fine. I thought you were still out with Trevor."

"No. He wanted to turn in early. The team has a practice tomorrow, and since his breakfast with the scouts, that's all he thinks about."

Sam couldn't bring herself to tell Mia the truth about JC and Mike. She trusted Case and would wait to see what he and Bobby could find out before she said something she'd regret.

"Listen, Mia. This whole baseball scout thing…you know not everybody gets picked up right away and…"

"I know, Mom. Trevor's excited, but I've already talked to him about it. He understands how things can go. I'm making sure he has his priorities straight. Don't worry."

Sam smiled. Mia was so much more mature than she needed to be at that age, and knowing what she knew about Trevor, the boy would need that voice of reason in his life, just like Case did when he was sixteen. She was glad Mia was there for him. Sam hugged her daughter tightly.

"Okay," Mia said, confused by the unexpected show of affection. "What was that for?"

"Just for being you, baby. But since we're both up, let's sit for a bit—just us women." Sam led Mia to the couch and sat beside her, holding her hand and looking her in the eyes. "Listen, honey, I know you sometimes have nightmares, and we've kinda been pretending everything is normal, but we both know it's not."

Mia looked down without speaking.

"I just want you to know that you don't have to be strong alone, okay? I am your mom, and now we have Case in our lives, and you know we'll always have your back."

Mia put on a brave face and nodded. "I know that, and

it's mostly fine—the bad dreams come and go, but it gets a little better every day. I love you, and I love Case. Plus, I've got Trevor and Dimpsey around. Having ya'll here helps me more than anything else—so I'll be okay. I promise. But thanks mom. It feels better just to talk about it sometimes."

Mia straightened up and kissed her mother on the cheek. Her loving smile was all Sam needed to see. "I think I'm going to go back to bed, okay?"

"Okay, sweetheart," Sam watched her daughter shuffle back down the hall before she got up and returned to her bedroom to find Case lying there asleep. He looked so peaceful and still. She knew the man had his demons, but to see him like this helped put her mind at ease. If Case could sleep so soundly knowing what he knew about JC, then so could she. Sam undressed and slipped under the covers next to Case. She felt safe there—like nothing could ever hurt her. Sam kissed him gently on his bare chest and closed her eyes. As long as she had Case by her side, she knew everything would be okay.

Chapter 30

After the wedding rehearsal, everyone sat around a big wooden table in the banquet hall of Maple Grove Golf Resort, laughing and enjoying each other's company. Amanda's parents had made it in from Medina, Ohio the night before and seemed genuinely happy to be adding Bobby to their family. Her mother, Joeann, listened with unabashed pride as Sam shared stories about their daughter's heroics on the police force, while Dimpsey entertained her dad, Cecil, with details about the ins and outs of cattle husbandry. Case's contribution to the conversation mainly involved embarrassing stories about Bobby from when they were young.

He told everyone how, one day after little league practice, eleven-year-old Bobby came home looking for something to quench his thirst. In the fridge, he found what he thought was a big mason jar full of fruit punch, but turned out to be the fermented starter for one of their mom's infamous friendship cakes. Bobby slammed the whole jar, and Molly came home to find the boy passed out drunk at the kitchen table. Their mom was appalled by the sight but their dad, Avis, had laughed hysterically before he gently carried Bobby to his room so he could sleep it off. To this day, Bobby couldn't look at a glass of fruit punch without wanting to throw up.

Amanda beamed as the bride-to-be and held Bobby's hand under the table as everyone went around, sharing their favorite memories and their excitement for the day to come. Case joined in as toasts were made and glasses were refilled, but in the back of his mind, he was still thinking about Wilks and Moretti. Case had made mistakes in the past by letting his temper get the best of him, but this time things were different. He just wanted to be left alone and craved peace in a way that only a man who had experienced the horrors of war could. He looked across the table at Dimpsey and wondered if he was feeling the same way.

After the rehearsal, the guests slowly went their separate ways. Bobby and Amanda headed home with her parents in tow while Trevor and Mia left for the movies, leaving Case, Sam, and Dimpsey to discuss their plan for the following day.

"So, did you hear back from Matt and Ross?" Sam inquired.

"Yes, I did. They'll be here before the wedding tomorrow."

"Good."

"But we still don't know much about our guests. All we know for sure is that these guys aren't who they say they are."

Dimpsey looked to Case, "What are we doing for firepower?"

"I'll be armed, along with Matt and Ross. Plus, Detective Wayne will be here for Bobby, so we can assume if anything happens, we'll have four guns in the fight."

"Five," Dimpsey said flatly.

There was the old warfighter Case's dad used to tell him stories about, "Fair enough, five guns in the fight."

"Make that six," Sam added. The determined look on her faced garnered no arguments from either Case or Dimpsey.

"What about Bobby?"

"That's up to him. It's his wedding day. I'm trying to keep this as unobtrusive as possible for him and Amanda. I'll be up front during the ceremony, so I'll have eyes on the crowd. Everyone else will sit behind or beside Moretti, Wilks, and Prissy, but with enough space to react if something goes wrong.

If that happens, we shut them down immediately."

Sam looked apprehensive. "Jesus, Case. If there's a chance this could go bad, wouldn't it be best just to postpone the wedding until these people are gone?"

"I would, Sam. But we have to know for sure whether or not this is tied to Grandview. If it is, and we don't handle it now, they'll just keep coming. Hopefully, I'm just being paranoid, and after the wedding, they all leave Pikesville for good."

Dimpsey nodded, "Pray for peace, but prepare for war." He said dolefully.

Case looked at his father's old friend. He did want peace—more than anything, but could never seem to find it. They'd all been through enough already and Case couldn't help but feel responsible. He had to keep JC close enough to shut him down quickly if things turned bad.

"That's right, Dimpsey. We have to be ready."

With that, the three said their goodbyes, but silently, Case considered if this could somehow be tied to Rex Kelley and the Dead Rebels. He hoped it wasn't, but as he and Sam pulled out of the gravel lot and onto the Blue Ridge Parkway, Dimpsey's words echoed in his head. *Pray for peace, but prepare for war.* It was time to prepare.

Back at the Motor Lodge, Prissy stood silently while JC went over his plan to firebomb the reception with Vince, Franco, and Mike.

Vince sat over a sketch he'd made of the reception area while JC stood over his shoulder, pointing out the main features of the dining hall.

"The main entrance is here," JC said, slamming his index

finger onto the paper. "It's closest to the parking lot, making it easier to slip out when the time comes. There are two more exits here and here." He said indicating the emergency exits inside the main hall and kitchen. "Prissy and I will wait for everyone to get settled. Once the food is served, I think everyone should stay put for a while. That's when me, Prissy and Mike will excuse ourselves. Vince, you and Franco will be standing by, ready to chain the doors."

Prissy shifted uncomfortably beside Mike, who placed his hand on her back.

"Then we toss the firebombs, wait until we know it's over, and leave. That's it."

"What about the fire department? Franco asked.

"This place is way out on the parkway. It'll take at least twenty minutes for anyone to get out there." Vince replied.

"And the fire suppression system?"

Vince pointed to a small "x" on the piece of paper, "I'll shut down the water main as soon as JC tells me when. Once the place is cookin' we'll monitor the windows from the parking lot to ensure no one makes it out of there alive."

Mike wanted nothing to do with it but reassured JC he would be there to deal with Case if he made it out of the building. That was the job, after all. A job that would finally get him out of debt and allow him to escape the tyranny of Tanner Greene once and for all. Prissy listened until she couldn't take it anymore. Sam, Amanda, and Crystal had accepted her as a friend and treated her like an equal, something she hadn't experienced since she was a little girl in Mississippi. The thought of them getting hurt was more than she could bear.

JC watched as she stormed into the next room. "Where the hell are you going?" He asked.

Prissy didn't respond but slammed the door between them. "Wait here,"

JC walked in to find Prissy packing her bag. "What the fuck do you think you're doing, Prissy?"

"I'm leaving JC. You told me you'd let me go if I helped you find Case. Well, I did what you wanted, and now I'm not going to hang around here and watch you kill my friends."

JC grabbed Prissy by the wrist. "You don't fucking leave until I say you leave. Got it?"

Prissy tried to jerk away but couldn't. JC was just too strong, so she lashed out instead. "Fine. You take me to that wedding, and I'll tell everyone what you're doing here. There's no way I just stand by and let you murder these people, JC. They haven't done anything to you."

JC swung Prissy against the wall and backhanded her hard across the face. "You little whore. These people *have* done something to me. They're standing in the way of what I want and now they'll die for it."

He dragged her back into the other room by the arm. Mike stood when he saw the blood running from the corner of Prissy's mouth. JC pointed at Mike with his free hand. "Don't be a fucking hero, Moretti."

Mike held his hands up and tried to defuse the situation. "Okay, JC. But there's no need to hurt one of our own."

"One of our own?" This little bitch just threatened to tell everyone what we're up to."

JC took a breath. "Change of plan. Mike, you and Franco are coming to the wedding with me. Vince, you're staying here and keeping an eye on this one. We might need her one more time." He said as he pushed Prissy across the room. "Once this is all done, I'll come back here and finish her myself."

As JC spoke to Vince and Franco, Prissy looked nervously at Mike, who shook his head almost imperceptibly—his eyes trying desperately to tell her it would all be okay. She knew he wouldn't let anything happen to her. Prissy tried to regain her composure. All she could do now was trust a man she barely knew, something she wasn't in the habit of doing. Mike lowered his hands and spoke softly to JC. "Whatever you say, boss."

That night, Prissy lay in bed with her arm cuffed to the brass headboard. She thought about Sam, Crystal, and Amanda as JC tossed restlessly beside her. She hated herself for ever believing such a horrible person would keep his word. He may not have been like the other bikers, but now, with a sober mind, Prissy saw the man for what he really was—a monstrous coward. In the past, she would have just accepted her fate without question. Her drug-addled mind being too focused on the next high to even consider her own value, but things were different now. She'd sobered up. Her mind was clear and sharp, and she was going to make JC regret the day he ever put a hand on her.

Chapter 31

It was late when they finally got back to the farm. Mia said goodnight and went to her room while Case and Sam sat on the porch swing, looking across the field toward Dimpsey's. Sam knew Case was struggling to keep himself in check—to not lose his temper and rush off to confront JC. She appreciated his attempt to keep everyone from panicking, but it was wearing on him, and she could tell.

"Case, are you okay?" She asked as she reached across and took his hand.

Case smiled and nodded. "I'm fine, Sam," but there was an emptiness in his eyes that she hated to see.

"Okay. We've had a long week. What do you say we go to bed?"

Case and Sam held hands as they walked down the hall to the bedroom, Sam undressed and slipped into her silk nightie while Case removed the pistol from his waistband and put it away in the big safe he'd installed in the closet. He was quiet and tense. After brushing his teeth and stripping down to his briefs, Sam watched him stop short of getting in the bed. He stood there silently for a while, then walked across the room and opened the safe again. Case unholstered the pistol he'd just put away and double-checked the mag and chamber before carrying it back to the bed and laying it on the nightstand beside him. He crawled under the covers and kissed Sam softly.

"I love you, Sam. Everything is going to be okay. I promise."

Case woke up to what felt like a madhouse. Sam sat in front of the small bedroom closet, tossing clothes aside as she searched for a lost shoe, while Mia yelled from the hallway.

"Mom, I need your hair straightener."

"You're either gonna have to wait or find it yourself, Mia. I'm looking for my other shoe."

Case sat in bed and stretched lazily, "What's all the fuss about? You'd think ya'll were late for a wedding or something."

"Oh, good morning, sunshine. Nice of you to join the living."

In reality, Case had barely slept. His mind had been too focused on JC and his reasons for being in Pikesville. "Seriously, why the hurry? The wedding isn't until this afternoon."

"I know, but Amanda wants to have brunch with all the bridesmaids before we start getting ready, so I need to have everything together before I leave the house…Mia! Are you dressed yet?"

"I'm gettin' there, mom, stop being such a spaz."

Case could see that Sam was struggling with more than finding her shoe, so he stood and walked across the room. He grabbed her by the shoulders and turned her toward him. "Sam, is everything alright?"

Tears formed in the corners of her eyes, but she didn't say anything.

"Talk to me, Sam."

Sam looked over at the gun on the nightstand, "What if this is about what happened in Grandview? I can't go through that again. It scares the hell out of me. I want to be supportive of you, Case. I really do, but I know you're worried about it too and I know how you'll react if things go bad."

"It's okay, Sam. We just have to be cautious. When I came

back home, I promised you that I'd never let anything happen to you or Mia again, and I meant that. But I can't lose my temper again and start tearing shit up like I did last time. It's reckless, and I feel horrible for having other people cover up my messes. I don't want to do that anymore. We don't know who these people are or what they want, so keeping them close to us is the best thing we can do for now."

Sam stepped back and wiped her eyes. She looked up and touched the jagged scar on the left side of Case's neck. "They almost killed you, Case."

Case hugged her tight as he thought back to the night everything went down in Grandview trailer park—the destruction he caused and the bullet he took to the neck. He wanted all that to stay in the past, but it haunted him. Case kissed Sam gently on the forehead, "But here I am, and we're all together. I'm not going to let anything jeopardize that. Okay?"

Sam looked into Case's deep blue eyes and relaxed in his arms. "Okay, Case. I believe you."

"Good. Now, would that happen to be your missing heel in the shoebox by the door?"

Sam rolled her eyes, smiling as she pushed away from Case and turned to grab the shoe, "Mia, Are you out of the bathroom yet?"

Mike played along with JC as best he could. He had serious doubts about Vince and Franco. He didn't trust either one of them to back his play. The best way to keep Prissy safe was to stay quiet and wait for his chance to get her clear of the motel. JC barked orders from the open door of the adjoining room.

"Vince, you'll be here keeping an eye on Prissy, but I want

all this shit packed up in the suburban so we can haul ass once this is done. Mike, Franco, we'll all be carrying sidearms at the wedding, but I want the long guns stashed in the back of the SUV, loaded and ready to go just in case. As soon as the deed is done, we come back here, take care of the girl, and head back to Richmond. Got it?"

"What do you mean by 'take care of the girl,' JC?" Mike asked.

JC stared at Mike as he reached into his back pocket and tossed a small zippered clutch purse to Vince. "What do you think I mean?"

Prissy recognized it as the stash bag where she kept her heroin and mainlining rig. JC had taken it from Detective Donaldson when he picked her up at the jail. Her heart sank at the thought of that shit ever entering her system again, and she started to cry.

"JC, please, no." She begged.

"Oh, fuck you, you little junkie. What did you think—I'd just turn you loose when this was all over so you could turn me in?"

Prissy pulled hard against the handcuffs that kept her attached to the bed. JC walked across the room and grabbed her by the face. "No, Prissy. You're going to die right here in this room, sad and shot up just like the rest of those little whores you used to call your friends."

JC pushed her face hard and looked at Mike, "Now get dressed. We have a fucking wedding to go to."

Chapter 32

Case and Sam pulled up at Maple Grove, followed closely by Trevor and Mia. The sky was blue and cloudless atop the rolling blue hills surrounding the lake. Strings of incandescent lights hung from the trees around the eighteenth hole to illuminate the evenings events. The big day had finally arrived and everyone was excited to get things underway. Case, however had more to worry about and was on edge, so he sent Sam inside with Mia and Trevor while he waited alone in the parking lot. Detective Wayne would stay with Bobby for the time being and perform the duties of the best man until the ceremony started. Dimpsey was the first to arrive. He stepped out of his beat-up Chevy Silverado wearing the only suit he owned. Case smiled and whistled.

Dimpsey looked uncomfortably at Case as he tugged at the knot in his tie. "You'd better hope this goes smooth today. Anything happens to this suit, and I won't have nothin' to be buried in."

"No funerals for you, Dimpsey. You're way too pretty to be sticking in the ground." Case teased.

Dimpsey huffed, "Where's the backup?"

"I just got a call from Ross. They'll be here any minute. The guests shouldn't be arriving for another couple of hours. That'll give us plenty of time to review our contingency plans. Did you ask around about our new guests?"

"I did and came back with nothing. Whoever these guys are, their focus is centered on us for some reason."

Case bit at his bottom lip. "You armed?"

Dimpsey slid his jacket aside to expose the grip of his Vietnam-era Colt M1911-A and a black leather belt stacked with extra mags of .45.

"Damn, Dimpsey. You come prepared."

"You know what they say about an ounce of prevention."

"That looks more like thirty-eight ounces of prevention to me."

Dimpsey was impressed that Case knew the exact weight of a fully loaded M1911, "You know your pistols, don't ya?"

"I know a little." Case heard the growl of an engine behind him and turned to see Matt and Ross pulling into the parking lot, driving an armored GMC Yukon XL. The vehicle was a beast and the go-to ride for the JTF's Critical Missions Project. Case had seen the SUV in action and knew what it was capable of.

"God all mighty." Dimpsey said under his breath as the big 420 hp, 6.2 liter, V8 rumbled toward him.

Case guided them into a reserved parking spot closest to the venue. He wanted certain people to see the vehicle, hoping it's presence would serve as a deterrent to trouble. Matt stepped out of the passenger side, looking every bit like a British spy in his fitted navy blue suit. Ross, on the other hand, walked around from the driver's seat looking ready for the beach in cut-off jean shorts, a Hawaiian shirt, and camouflage Crocks.

"What the hell, Ross? You thought you were attending a luau?" Case joked.

"Hey, these are my driving clothes. I'll look just as sharp as Rico Suave here as soon as I change."

"Well, hop to it, Magnum. We have things to do."

Case had known Matt and Ross for almost a decade. They'd

met soon after Case reported to the Philadelphia Field Office and immediately became fast friends. Both men were combat vets; Matt had been Army infantry like Case and Ross a former Marine Corps sniper. They were smart, stayed fit, and were dedicated to the mission. Once Case made team leader in Philly, Matt, and Ross were the first two names added to his roster, and he was glad he did. There were no two men he'd rather have on his side in a fight.

The plan was to set up concentric rings of security around the outdoor venue to control JC and whoever was with him. Case and Ross met guests in the parking lot and pointed them toward the wedding, while Matt and Dimpsey greeted them at the large wooden arbor that marked the entrance and showed them to their seats. Once the wedding was over, guests would be escorted to the banquet hall for the reception and again given specific seating, keeping JC somewhat isolated and surrounded. After the reception, guests would be invited back out to the lakeside for music and dancing.

Mike Moretti drove up in their rented suburban with JC in the passenger seat. Someone else sat in the back, but it wasn't Prissy. Case greeted them as they stepped from the vehicle, getting close enough to take a quick peek inside. He noted nothing out of the ordinary.

"Hey Mike, how are ya?" Case said, taking the former SEAL's hand.

"Good, and you?"

"Doing well, thanks. Is Prissy coming in a separate vehicle?"

JC spoke up from the passenger side. "Prissy was feeling a little under the weather this morning. She won't be joining us today, and wanted me to pass along her apology."

Case knew the man was lying, "That's too bad, the girls will be disappointed. I hope she's okay."

The third person stepped out of the back, and Case immediately recognized him as one of the men he'd spotted standing along the outfield fence during Trevor's game. *This is not shaping up well*, he thought.

"And you are?" Case asked, careful to keep the smile on his face.

The stranger stuck his hand out, but JC stepped in and made the introduction.

"Case, this is Franco Mendoza. He's an associate of mine from the university. Since Prissy couldn't make it, I thought it would be okay to bring him along. I hope that's alright."

Case shook the man's hand, eying him cautiously. "Of course. It's always nice to see another friendly face in the crowd. Now, if you guys wouldn't mind, just head toward the lake, and my friend Matt will show you to your seats."

After they all walked away, Ross, now transformed by a slate gray Tom Ford suit, stood next to Case.

"Well?"

Case watched as Matt and Dimpsey greeted the men and showed them to their seats. All three eyed the big armored Yukon as they made their way toward the lake. "This is off. All three of those guys are lying to us.

"What's the play?"

"We stick with the plan. Once all the guests are seated, I'll take the best man's spot up front. Matt and Dimpsey will be seated around those three while Detective Wayne stands at the entrance. You'll be out here in the parking lot as overwatch. Anything looks amiss, and we get those three clear of the guests as fast as we can."

"Got it, boss," Ross said as he took his post beside the Yukon. Case walked down the slope toward the venue just as the music began to play. It was showtime.

Chapter 33

The hard steel cuffs cut into Prissy's wrist as she lay on the bed watching an old rerun of the Andy Griffith show. She remembered it from when she was a kid in Mississippi—the episode where Deputy Barney Fife, and Floyd, the barber, get lured to a remote cabin by two women who turned out to be escaped convicts. She understood what they were going through, but didn't think her situation was quite as funny. Vince sat quietly at the table by the door, working a crossword puzzle from the newspaper he'd picked up at the gas station across the street.

"Would it be too much to ask for a glass of water?" Prissy enquired.

Looking slightly irritated, Vince stood up without speaking and walked to the bathroom counter, where he filled a plastic cup with water from the sink. With Vince out of the way, Prissy could see the newspaper and Skilcraft ballpoint pen lying on the table's edge less than ten feet away. There had to be a way to get Vince out of the room long enough to get her hands on that pen.

Vince handed Prissy the water and sat back down. "Ya know what sounds good?" Prissy asked after a few minutes of silence.

"What?" Vince said, slamming the newspaper back on the table.

"One of those Payday bars from the vending machine out front. Mike had one the other day, and it looked really good."

Vince rolled his eyes in frustration.

"Please, Vince, I haven't eaten all day. I'm cuffed to a

damned bed for God's sake, so how about you quit being an asshole and just get me a candy bar…please."

Vince sat the pen down beside the newspaper again and walked outside, digging in his pocket for change. Prissy waited until she knew he was clear of the room and made her move. She stood and grabbed the edge of the bed, pulling as hard as she could on the frame to move closer to the table. It only took a few seconds before she had her hands on the pen.

Once, during a lockup at county, she'd learned to shim a set of handcuffs from one of the older prostitutes. She only needed the thin metal pocket clip from Vince's government-issued Skilcraft pen. Prissy broke the clip off quickly and shoved the flat end into the first cuff between the teeth and the lock housing, just like she'd been taught. JC and Vince hadn't thought to double-lock the cuffs, so opening them up was easy. Once free, she looked out the window to see Vince walking back toward the room. *Think Priscilla.* Moving as quickly as she could, Prissy unplugged the small microwave on the dresser and hid behind the door.

Vince walked inside, but by the time he noticed the bed had been moved, it was too late. Prissy came down hard on the man's head with the microwave. Blood poured from a gash in his scalp as he crashed to the floor unconscious. Prissy searched the man's pockets and found a cell phone and a wallet with $220 cash in it. Prissy set those aside, then took the Glock 19 from Vince's waistband. After that, she finished removing her cuffs and secured the unconscious man to the bed, closed the blinds, and disconnected the room phone, taking the cord with her. She needed to warn Sam about JC if she expected her friends to survive.

Chapter 34

The midday sun danced lazily across Maple Grove Lake as everyone stood and turned toward the reception area. Amanda stepped out looking stunning in her fairytale-style dress, with its sweetheart neckline, layers of airy tulle, and ornately embroidered lace. Her dad, Cecil, beamed at her side as he escorted his baby girl to the front of the small crowd and handed her over to Bobby. Case noticed that Bobby was holding his breath so he put a hand on his little brother's shoulder.

"Breathe, Bobby." Case whispered.

Once Bobby regained his composure, the wedding went off without a hitch. Amanda beamed as Bobby recited his vows, then gasped aloud when he slipped his grandmother's wedding ring onto her finger. It was a simple golden band with a large, sparkling diamond set in the center. Their grandfather, Carl, had brought it home from Germany after the war. When they were married, he gave it to his fiancé, Edna, and she'd handed it down to their daughter, Molly, hoping she would one day have a son.

Case watched the gathering vigilantly as the small crowd stood and cheered when Bobby kissed the bride. Dillon Wayne stayed close by as Mr. and Mrs. Younger held hands and ran joyfully past the guests, who threw handfuls of rice over their heads. Case had never seen his little brother so happy.

Once Bobby and Amanda disappeared into the reception area, the crowd started breaking up, shaking hands and catching up with old friends as they slowly made their way to the banquet hall. Case made eye contact with Matt and Dimpsey, who closed in on JC, Mike, and Franco, but as they walked up the slope, Franco split off and headed back toward the parking lot. Case pulled out his phone and shot a quick text to Ross.

"One moving your way. Keep an eye on him. We have the other two in sight."

"Roger that, boss," came the reply.

Ross leaned against the hood of the Yukon with his arms crossed, watching the last of the guests enter the banquet hall as Franco approached the parking lot.

"Hey, buddy. You forget something?"

"Just gotta grab a couple of things out of the car," Franco said as he continued to the rented suburban. Ross relinquished his post and followed closely behind.

"I'd be happy to give you a hand if ya need it. I'm way stronger than I look."

When Franco opened the back hatch of the suburban, Ross saw a partitioned box full of glass bottles. They were filled with an amber liquid and plugged with strips of torn cloth. Ross knew exactly what they were, and that they had no place at a wedding. Then, he saw the chains, padlocks and the butt of an AR-15 and knew things were about to go bad. "Yeah, that looks pretty heavy. You're definitely gonna need some help."

Franco turned and swung, but Ross was ready. He raised his left hand and placed it behind his neck, using the bent arm to protect his head from the blow. With his right, he punched the man hard in the sternum. Franco doubled over and fought to catch his breath. Ross set himself up for the finishing blow, but Franco lashed out wildly. Ross didn't realize he'd been cut until he looked down and saw the blood slowly seeping through his white dress shirt just above the breast pocket.

"Fuck, man! That's my good shirt."

Franco lunged again, which was what Ross had expected. He blocked the blow with the outside of his forearm to avoid any major arteries, then trapped the knife with his other hand, pinning it against his hip—a move he'd rehearsed thousands of times as a Federal Air Marshal. Franco's only choice now was to swing with the other arm. When he did, Ross ducked under the blow and rotated his body, hyperextending Franco's elbow and stripping the knife from his grasp. The look on Franco's face said it all. It was over.

"Ya didn't expect that, did ya?" Ross said as he grabbed the back of Franco's head and drove the knife down hard behind the man's left collarbone, severing the subclavian artery. Franco's eyes went wide as he staggered backward and then slumped against the hatch of the suburban.

Ross stepped in close as blood pumped rhythmically from the hole in Franco's neck. "It's okay, buddy. It'll all be over soon."

Once everyone was safely inside, Case stood at the head table overlooking the crowd. Dimpsey sat JC and Mike in the corner near the exit to keep some space between them and the rest of the guests. Their relative isolation made it easier for Case to keep an eye on them and to react should anything go wrong. Everything was going according to plan, and since the wedding went smoothly, Case was starting to relax a bit—then his phone rang.

Case looked down to see Andre Brown's number on the screen.

"Andre. This is unexpected."

Never one to mince words, Andre got straight to the point, "Case, you've got a big problem down there."

"How so?"

"Matt told me about your unexpected guests, so I took it upon myself to search the digital evidence you guys retrieved from that last hit. Specifically, the thumb-drive you guys pulled off our friend Reggie Stansfield. This guy, Wilks, is all over it. He may have a clean criminal record, but it turns out he's a fully patched member of the Dead Rebels Motorcycle Club. He's the one they put in charge to establish trafficking routes through that area, and the only reason he would have to be in Pikesville is you."

Now everything clicked into place. Case felt his face redden and his fist clench around the phone as he stared at JC from across the room. That night in Richmond, he'd locked five Dead Rebel's inside the Rusty Spoke before setting the place on fire. It looks like the sixth had come to find his revenge. As for the girl, Prissy, she'd put on a little weight and cleaned herself up, but it was definitely her—the girl from outside the bar that night. The one he'd sent away.

"He's also tied to a much larger trafficking organization being run out of New York." Andre continued. "The man in charge is a financière by the name of Tanner Greene."

Case remembered Detective Wayne mentioning Greene when he ran Mike Moretti through NCIC, the National Crime Information Center.

"This guy Greene's connected at the highest levels of government and business, but trust me, Case, he's the worst of the bunch. You need me to send you some more guys?"

"No." Case said before hanging up, "Thank you, Andre. It's a little late for that, but I'm gonna handle this right now."

As guests slowly found their way to their seats and the head table started to fill, Sam sat close to Amanda, admiring her ring. She tried to get Case's attention by tugging at his suit coat, but his focus wasn't on the reception. His eyes were locked on JC and Mike in the back of the room

"Case, what's wrong?"

Like Sam, Dimpsey saw the shift in Case's demeanor and knew things were about to turn bad. He grabbed Sam and Amanda by the shoulders. "Get out now! I'll grab Mia and Trevor."

Just then, Ross burst through the door, his shirt torn and bloody. Case saw the look of shock on JC's face as he realized his plan was blown. In a panic, JC stood, drew the pistol he had stashed in the small of his back, and fired wildly in Case's direction.

Part Three

Fallout

Chapter 35

The first round went wide, striking the wall just to the left of Case's head. The second round caught Crystal in the right leg just above her knee. She went down hard, screaming. The crowd stood in shock as their minds tried to process what was happening, some were frozen, unable to scream or react. Others resorted to self-preservation, fleeing the scene as fast as they could, leaving their loved ones to fend for themselves. A select few sprang into action, shielding others as their eyes scanned the room to pinpoint the source of danger. Case crouched slightly as he drew the Glock 19 from his waistband and moved quickly toward the threat, weapon extended, sights in alignment, resting steadily on the center of JC's face. Just as he began squeezing the trigger, his target disappeared.

Damn it!

Case brought the weapon back to the high-ready position in the center of his chest to give himself a better field of view. That's when he saw Mike struggling with JC, fighting for control of the gun he'd fired at Case. As Matt, Ross, and Detective Wayne jumped in, JC pulled away and sprinted toward the exit. By the time Case could close the distance, JC was gone, but Mike was pinned to the floor, struggling against the three men it took to hold him there. Case jumped into the fray and pressed the muzzle of his Glock into the center of Mike's forehead. Mike could see the look in Case's eyes and knew that fighting back would only result in his head being split in two, so he stopped.

"Case don't shoot me. I didn't want things to come to this. I tried to stop him."

Case pressed the weapon down harder, "You've got about two seconds to tell me everything I need to know, or you die right here on the floor. What the fuck are you doing in Pikesville?"

Mike didn't hesitate, "JC's a member of the Dead Rebels. He was away in New York working with a man named Tanner Greene the night you burned that bar down in Richmond. Greene wants his business back up and running through Pikesville, and you're an obstacle to that."

Everything Case was hearing lined up with what he'd just learned for Andre Brown. "And?"

"He sent me down here with a couple of other guys to back JC and get you out of the picture, but JC wanted to prove a point. He wanted to burn you and the rest of these people down just like you did his friends. I wasn't on board with that Case. I swear I tried to stop him."

Case could see that Mike was being truthful, but he still couldn't be trusted. He stood up, jerking Mike violently to his feet. "Where will he go now?"

"Vince is at the motel keeping an eye on Prissy. She's innocent in all this, Case. She threatened to tell you and Sam about JC's plan as soon as she found out about it. That's why she's not here. Franco's waiting in the parking lot for JC. They'll head back to the motel to pick up Vince and get rid of Prissy. Then the three of 'em will come after you."

"Your friend Franco won't be going anywhere," Ross said as he sat inspecting the deep gash that ran across his chest.

Case held Mike by the back of his collar as Matt and Detective Wayne stood and ushered the crowd away from the scene.

Case looked over at Mia, standing in the corner beside her friends, eyes wide, a look of complete shock on her face.

"Mia, are you okay?" he asked.

Mia's mouth hung open as she glanced toward the door.

Dimpsey looked frantically around the room, "Mia! Where's Trevor?"

"He went outside to get my jacket from the truck," she said in a daze.

Case saw the look on Dimpsey's face and knew things had just gotten substantially worse, "Dimpsey, I'll go find Trevor, okay? I need you to get Sam, Mia, and Amanda out of here. Take them back to your place. Arm up and shelter there until you hear back from me."

Every fiber of Dimpsey's being wanted to protest. He wanted to take the fight to JC the same way he would have when he was younger, but knew he couldn't, "Okay, Case. Just don't let anything happen to my boy."

Case felt the weight of the situation pressing down on him and fought against it. Now was not the time to lose his temper. He needed to stay in control.

"I won't Dimpsey. I promise, but we have to move now. Bobby, I need you and Dillon to call this in and get backup out here immediately." Case would rather have had Bobby with him, but was more concerned about having police present at the scene to coordinate a response and take care of the wedding guests.

Bobby looked distraught. "What about Amanda?"

"She'll be safe with Dimpsey. He'll take care of her until we get this mess sorted out."

Bobby was reluctant but agreed.

Case looked over at Ross, who was bleeding profusely now

that the adrenaline was wearing off. "Matt, get Ross and Crystal to the hospital and get them taken care of. Keep your phone on. If I need you, I'll call, but get those two situated first."

"Copy that. What are you gonna do?"

Case shoved Mike toward the door, "Me and my new best friend here are going after JC."

"You think having him around is a good idea?" Wayne asked. "I can secure him here till backup arrives."

"Mike knows JC's plan, and what he'll do next, so I need him for now. Trust me, as soon as I'm done with him, he's all yours."

Mike spoke up. "I want to help, Case. JC's lost his mind, and he's plannin' on killin' Prissy. I want him dead just as bad as you do. You don't have to worry about me."

"You're gonna prove that or die trying,"

Matt stopped Case before he could leave. "Here, take this," he said, handing Case the keys to the CMP's Yukon. "You'll need it more than I do. There's guns and gear in the back. Take whatever you need."

Case reached into his pocket and tossed the keys to his dad's old truck over to Matt, "You take mine."

Matt held the keys up as Case walked Mike out the door, "Not exactly a fair trade, but you're welcome."

Once in the parking lot, Case released Mike, and the two men faced each other.

"Case, I—"

"Don't," Case interrupted. "This goes one of two ways. You help me get to JC without any problems, or I take you down just like I did the rest of them. The choice is yours."

Mike knew enough about Case to see that the man was serious and capable of doing precisely what he said.

"You'll get no trouble from me. I swear it. Right now, I'm only worried about gettin' Priscilla away from JC before it's too late."

Case looked around the parking lot but saw no sign of Trevor or his truck. He stared back at Mike, his eyes cold and indifferent. It seemed JC had put them both in the same position, something Case could use to his advantage. "Get in the car."

Chapter 36

Back in her room, Prissy searched frantically for the phone number Sam had written down for her when they'd met at the bar. She dumped her purse onto the bed and finally found it folded and stashed in one of the small zippered pockets. Then, she repacked the bag with the phone, wallet, and gun she'd taken from Vince and ran from the room. On the way out, she noticed another set of keys lying on the table next to the door—JC's bright red Audi R8.

"Oh, hell yes! Thanks, JC."

"Pick up, pick up, pick up," Prissy shouted into the cellphone as she sped down Route 221 away from the motel. She didn't know where she was going but knew she needed to get as far away as possible and that Sam had to be warned. Finally, someone answered.

"Hello."

"Sam, it's Prissy. Are you okay?"

"Barely," Sam shouted, obviously furious. "Your fiancé just tried to kill us at the wedding reception, Prissy. What the hell is happening?"

Prissy didn't know where to begin. "He's not my fiancé, Sam. I'm being held against my will. I tried to stop him. I told him I was going to tell you everything, and he cuffed me to the bed so I couldn't. He's going to kill me, then go after Case. We have to stop him, Sam. I don't want anything to happen to you."

Sam was silent.

"Sam, please. You have to believe me. We're all in danger."

Sam looked out the passenger window of Dimpsey's old Silverado, soothed by the blur of green as they sped past the treelined roads leading to the farm. She knew the girl had to have known about JC's plan, but didn't say anything to her about it. In the back of her mind, Sam realized Prissy had only done what she had to protect herself from JC. Now, she was on the run and scared as hell. Sam wanted to help but didn't want Prissy near Mia or Amanda until she could speak to her alone and figure out what was happening.

"Okay. I'm gonna text you an address. Get there as quickly as you can."

"Okay…and, Sam," Prissy sobbed, "I'm really sorry. Meeting you and your friends was the best thing to happen to me in a long time. I never wanted any of this."

Sam could hear the heartbreak in Prissy's voice and sensed she was telling the truth, "Just get to the address I sent you, okay. We'll figure things out from there." She said before hanging up.

Mia sat squeezed between Amanda and Sam, as Dimpsey raced toward home. "Was that that girl, Mom?"

"Yes, it was."

"You're not gonna help her, are you?"

Sam considered why she felt compelled to help. All she knew right now was that Prissy was a woman in need and afraid for her life. She couldn't turn her back on someone in that position. "Mia, you know how difficult things were last year when those bikers took you. Well, those things and worse have been happening to that girl every day for a very long time and we are not gonna let that continue."

Mia knew her mother was doing the right thing, "Okay, mom. I understand."

Sam patted Mia on the knee, "Dimpsey, I need you to drop me off at the farm, then take Mia and Amanda to your place. I'll meet you there."

Chapter 37

JC burst into the motel room and shoved Trevor onto the floor.

"Stay put you little shit."

JC looked around expecting to find things as he'd left them but Prissy was nowhere in sight. The room looked like it had been ransacked and Vince sat cuffed to the bed, rubbing a massive lump on his bloody head.

"What the fuck, Vince."

Vince looked at his blood-covered hand and groaned.

"I'm sorry, JC. I went to get something from the vending machine out front, and when I got back, she was out of the cuffs and blindsided me with a microwave."

JC pulled the curtains apart and looked into the parking lot, "And she took my car, you useless asshole!"

"She has everything, JC. My gun, phone, cash…"

"God damn it!" JC screamed as he fished around in his pocket for the cuff key. "You're a real fucking tough-guy, aren't ya? The only person I have left on this fucking crew and you let yourself get bested by a hundred-and-ten-pound girl."

After releasing Vince from his restraints, JC stormed across the room, "Get your shit together. We have work to do."

"What happened at the wedding?"

"What do you think?"

"You just said I'm the only one left. Where's Mike and Franco?"

JC paced the room, infuriated that his plans had fallen

apart so quickly. "Franco got made in the parking lot, now he's dead. The same thing almost happened to me, thanks to your faithless fucking boss."

Vince was shocked and a little saddened to hear that Franco was dead. Despite all the big talk, he'd never really lost a friend in combat. Hell, he'd never really been in combat. The realization that he could meet the same fate hit Vince like a stone. He wasn't ready for this.

"What happened with Mike?"

"Somehow Franco got busted and Case figured things out just as the reception was starting. I was going to take Younger out myself, but Mike jumped me. I got away and was able to snatch this little shithead on my way out." JC said pointing to Trevor, "The last thing I saw was Case and his buddies piling onto Mike. I don't know what happened after that, but I hope they killed the prick."

"What do we do now? Should we call Tanner?"

"No!" JC screamed. "We fucking handle this ourselves. You say a word to Greene and I shoot you myself."

Vince stopped asking questions and sat quietly as JC tried to figure out their next step.

"What do we have stashed in Tanner's suburban out back?" JC asked.

"A couple of ARs and about 12 mags of .556. The rest was in the rental."

"That's all gone now. Whatever's in the Suburban is all we have."

"It's not going to be enough, ya know," Trevor said as he sat up on the floor. "Case'll run right over you if you try to hurt anybody here in Pikesville."

JC picked Trevor up by his collar and slapped him hard

across the face. "You keep your fucking mouth shut, kid."

Trevor had never been hit by a grown man before. His eyes watered, but he didn't let the pain show. Instead, he smiled maliciously at JC through blood smeared lips.

"Fuckin' little asshole. They'll more than likely head to Case's place next. We need to get there first. I have the address from Donaldson. Get this kid secured and put him in the suburban. We have to get moving."

Vince used the cuffs from the bed to secure Trevor's hands behind his back and sat him on the couch. "I'll go get the SUV and park in front of the room so we're not marching this kid across the parking lot."

"Just get moving. We don't have much time."

With that, Vince walked out the door and around the back to get the Suburban as JC paced the room. Trevor watched from the couch without speaking. He knew what Case had done to the guys who took Mia last year. He knew that no matter what, Case wouldn't let anything happen to him. All he had to do was be patient and keep his mouth shut.

Mike knew he'd screwed up. Now that JC's plan was blown, he knew he'd burnt all his bridges. In some ways it was a relief. The only bright side to the whole thing had been Prissy and he knew what would happen if JC got to her first. Mike looked over at Case as he sped along the Blue Ridge Parkway toward Pikesville and decided to risk speaking.

"Case I—"

"Don't! You son of a bitch. I trusted you around my family. All I need from you now is to know where JC's headed and what he's planning. Once I have him, you get handed over to the police."

"I get that. I want JC gone just as bad as you do, so I'll take whatever I have coming. But you need to know what you're up against, and you need to know that Prissy had nothing to do with this. She's in trouble, Case, and I don't want to see her hurt. So, let me help you save these people, and when this is done, I'll go to the police myself."

Case looked at Mike and saw nothing but sincerity in his eyes. He couldn't trust the man, but he needed the help at this point, and Mike was the one closest to JC and his crew. "Tell me what he'll do next."

Mike relaxed a bit. "JC's dangerous, but he's also a coward. He'll only go head-to-head with someone he knows he can beat, or if he has the upper hand. Otherwise, he needs backup. Vince is at the motel watching Prissy. He'll go there first to get Vince, then go after your friends to draw you out. But he'll kill Prissy first. He considers her too big of a liability."

"What kind of firepower does he have?"

"A lot of what he had was in the rented SUV he brought to the wedding, but he has one of Stonehill's vehicles back at the motel. It had a couple of ARs and some mags in it. They'll have that and their sidearms. Nothing heavier though."

"Nothing long-range?"

"They're no good past three hundred meters. What do you have?"

"My Glock and the Sig P365 I took off you." Case said, looking over at Mike with hate in his eyes. "The pistol you planned to use to kill me and my family."

Mike didn't know how to respond, so he chose honesty, "The only person I was there for was you, Case. The rest was on JC. You were the job—nobody else. And the only reason that job existed in the first place is because you murdered those men in that bar."

Case knew he was the cause of all this, but chose not to acknowledge it. "Tell me more about Stonehill and Tanner Greene."

"Greene's just some rich asshole that gave me work after I got booted from the SEAL teams and pulled my time in Leavenworth. All of which I'm sure you already know."

Case nodded, "And?"

"Tanner made me the head of his security detail. He likes to feel more important than he is, and for the most part, that's all I did was security. But occasionally, Tanner would call on me for other things. Like getting rid of you."

"And why did Tanner Greene want to come after me?"

"That's where JC comes in. Tanner has some shady shit going on within his business. Namely transporting and selling young women."

Case's knuckles turned white as he clutched the steering wheel.

"JC was in New York negotiating a deal between the Rebels and Tanner the night you burned that bar down. It looked like a standard courier deal on paper, but it was just a method to move girls from Richmond through JC's home city of Baltimore and up into New York. Most of those girls were coming from areas like Pikesville, but you were the monkey wrench nobody expected. Tanner was afraid a man like you would expose him and his business so he wanted you out of the picture. Once I found out JC was after more than just you, I didn't want any part of it. Getting rid of you was supposed to be my last job with Tanner."

"A man with your background has options, Mike. Why did

you agree to any of this?"

"Because it offered me a chance to clear some debts I owed."

"Gambling?" Case asked.

"No," Mike said looking down at the floorboard, "My mother's medical bills."

Case saw that Mike was hurting and actually felt for the man but didn't respond right away. Instead, he leaned forward, retrieved the P365 he had stashed in the small of his back, and sat the pistol on the seat of the Yukon between him and Mike.

"Life's about the choices we make, Mike, and God knows I've made some bad ones. I know enough about you to know you learned that lesson the hard way, just like I did. We both have a chance to make it right this time. So, let's not fuck it up."

Mike knew his life had been a mess. He needed something to reverse some of the damage he'd done the same way Case did. If fighting alongside the man he was sent to kill would save Prissy, then so be it. He was all in. Case kept a grip on the Glock 19 lying in his lap and watched as Mike reached across the seat and took the pistol. He performed a quick press check, then dropped the mag and made sure it was topped off before reinserting it and tugging on the floorplate. Mike stuck the weapon in his waistband and sat back without saying anything else. No words would be sufficient. It was time to prove his worth.

Chapter 38

Prissy pulled up at the address Sam had sent her. The farmhouse was small but sturdily built with a fresh coat of paint and what looked like new fencing all the way around. Newly planted flowers surrounded the trees out front, and Prissy could see where someone had started work on a covered swing that faced the blue/gray mountains lying to the west. It wasn't just a house but a home—something Prissy hadn't been a part of since she left Mississippi. Sam stood on the porch with her arms crossed, waiting impatiently.

"Sam, I'm so sorry," Prissy cried as she stepped out of JC's Audi. "I never meant—"

"Stop it, Prissy," Sam interrupted, I don't care what you meant. You need to be upfront with me right now and tell me exactly what's happening with JC."

"He's a monster, Sam."

"I knew that the moment he shot Crystal. But I need to know why he's doing it and how we can stop him."

Prissy looked shocked, "He shot Crystal?" Tears streamed down her face as she walked toward Sam. "Is she okay?"

"She'll be fine, but I need to know what's happening, and I need to know now, Prissy. We're not safe here with JC running around Pikesville, so please tell me what the hell is going on."

Prissy stood at the foot of the steps leading to the porch and looked up at Sam, "None of us have any business here. JC's not who he says he is Sam. I never meant to put anyone in this position."

"Who is he Prissy, and why is he here?"

Prissy looked crestfallen, "He's the Sergeant at Arms for the Dead Rebels out of Richmond."

Sam felt her heart sink at the mention of the gang. "Do you know what they did here last year?"

"No. Not really. But I remember Case from that night in Richmond."

"What do mean? What happened in Richmond Prissy?"

Prissy didn't know where to begin. "I don't know much. I was so high. All I know is Case showed up at the hangout. He told me to walk away and I did. Then…"

Sam watched as Prissy grappled with what to say next. "What, Prissy? What did Case do?"

Prissy stared at Sam before answering, "All I know is, after Case told me to leave, the place burned down." The girl's mind replayed what little she could remember. It was not a good memory. "I could hear them screaming from way up the street. Everybody but JC was trapped inside. Nobody made it out."

Sam knew what Case was capable of and that he sometimes withheld things in order to protect her and Mia. She also knew she was on his side, no matter what.

"So, JC's here for revenge."

Prissy hung her head, "He promised that if I helped him, he'd let me go. Sam, I just wanted to be free from the club. You, Crystal, and Amanda are the only friends I've ever known. I didn't mean for any of this to happen."

Sam thought about what would have happened to Mia had Case not been there for her and could feel her heart breaking for Prissy. She knew the girl wasn't responsible; she was a victim, and whether she knew it or not, she was free now. Sam intended to keep it that way.

"Okay," Sam said as she stepped off the porch and wrapped her arms around Prissy, "It's going to be okay. Case will stop this. I promise."

Sam could feel Prissy sobbing in her arms and looked toward the dust cloud speeding along the road that led into the farm. "Someone's coming, Prissy. Did you tell anyone where you were going?"

"No, but JC knows about this place."

Sam's face turned grim, "We need to get you inside, now."

Chapter 39

Case burst into the motel room with his gun up, followed closely by Mike. Each cleared their respective corners and swept the room from left to right, ensuring no one was inside. On the ride over, Mike had described the layout of the rooms and told Case about the adjacent door, which stood open to the left. Case signaled for Mike to check it while he covered the bathroom door on the far side of the room. Mike stayed close to the wall with his P365 fully extended, looking as deep into the corner of the next room as he could without exposing himself. Then, slowly and methodically, he side-stepped to the right, revealing slivers of the adjoining room until he made his way to the opposite side of the door. Once he'd cleared as much as he could, he stepped quickly inside the room with his pistol pointed into the blind corner, then swung right again to check the opposite side, "Clear," he shouted to Case. Once in position, both men moved toward the back of the rooms in unison and searched the two small bathrooms. They came up empty.

With both rooms secured, Case and Mike met back in the center.

"What do you think?" Case asked.

"There's blood on the floor where they were keeping Prissy, and the bed's been drug into the center of the room. Trevor's truck is outside, so given that both the Suburban and JC's Audi are missing, it looks like Prissy might have gotten away."

Case weighed his options.

"He knows where the farm is?"

"He does."

"Then we need to move now. I sent everyone across the road to Dimpsey's, so the house will be empty when he gets there. I doubt we can beat him to it, but we still might be able to get the drop on him if we hurry."

"I'll follow your lead," Mike said as he tucked the P365 back into his waistband.

Case could tell he was serious about getting to JC before any more damage was done, especially to Prissy.

"Okay then. Let's get moving."

Once back at home, Dimpsey immediately started emptying the gun cabinet. He didn't know if the fight would make its way across the road, but he wanted to be prepared. Mia and Amanda watched from the doorway as Dimpsey stacked an assortment of pistols, rifles, and ammo cans in the center of the living room.

"You know how to shoot one of these?" Dimpsey asked Mia as he pointed to the Henry lever action 30-30 lying on the coffee table. It was a big weapon with a dark wooden stock and heavy octagonal barrel.

Mia shook her head but didn't say anything.

"Look," Dimpsey grabbed the rifle and put it against Mia's shoulder. "Just look down the barrel. Put the painted dot on the top of the front sight right down in this notch. Then, put that on whatever it is you're tryin' to shoot. Once that's all lined up, just squeeze the trigger."

Mia nodded.

"Once it fires, you'll have to work this lever to get another round in the chamber, okay? Then just keep doin' that till it's empty. When it goes dry, you holler for me."

"Okay, Mister Campbell," Mia said as she worked up her confidence. "I can handle it."

"Okay, good. Now, I'll load all these up. You and Amanda start stackin' 'em by the windows facin' the road. Anybody comes this way you let me know."

Amanda went to work but noticed the look of terror on Mia's face. The girl had been through so much over the past year—the kidnapping, the assault on her mom, and the murder of her biological father. She couldn't even imagine what the girl must be feeling right now.

"Hey." Amanda said, placing her hand on Mia's shoulder, "You okay?"

"Yeah. I'm okay. I just wish Mom was back."

"She'll be here, sweetie. In the meantime, it's important that we do what Dimpsey says, okay? Hopefully, Case gets to these guys first, and we'll never have to fire a shot, but it's best that we be ready."

"Yeah. I've got this," Mia said as she took the 30-30 from Dimpsey and stood by the window next to the entrance. It reminded her of the last stand of the Regulators from the movie Young Guns that she'd watched with Case. Only this time, she hoped all the good-guys made it out alive.

Chapter 40

JC saw his Audi parked in front of the farmhouse and stopped before pulling into the long gravel driveway. He saw no movement inside or around the house.

"Okay, how do you want to approach this?" Vince asked from the passenger seat.

JC studied the layout of the farm, taking note of the large barn in the back and the natural cover and concealment available around the house. "We don't know who or what is up there, so we need to be careful." JC turned to Trevor, who sat cuffed in the backseat, "What's in the barn, kid?"

"Nothing. It's just full of old hay and a few tools. Case uses it as a garage mostly."

"How many guns does Case have in the house?"

"None that I know of," Trevor lied.

"Okay. I don't know if you're telling the truth or not, but we'll find out. And if you're lying, you'll be the first one to die today, you got that?"

Trevor stared defiantly at JC but didn't say anything else.

"Vince, pull the car up parallel to the road so we block off the driveway. Load up the ARs and grab the mags. I'll get the kid."

Vince did as he was told. JC jumped out of the Suburban and snatched Trevor from the back seat. "Let's go, kid. Time to move."

Sam peeked through the front room curtains and looked down the driveway. Huge Red Maples stood in the yard, obstructing her view, but she could still make out the silhouette of a large black SUV parked by the road.

"Prissy, is that them?"

Priscilla rushed to Sam's side. "Shit! That's JC and Vince."

Sam tried to keep her composure as she watched JC shove someone up the road in front of him. It felt like a truck hit her when she realized it was Trevor.

Prissy started to panic, "Sam, JC will kill that kid if it means getting to Case."

Sam turned to face Prissy and grabbed the girl by her shoulders, "Well, we're not gonna let that happen, Prissy. Do you know how to shoot a gun?"

Case and Mike sped along Route 100 on their way to the farm. Dimpsey could handle the situation until they got there, but he knew there wasn't much time. Mike's body pitched forward as Case slammed on the brakes and slid to a stop.

"Look," Case said, pointing ahead to the entrance of the Younger property.

Mike saw the black Suburban parked sideways in the driveway, blocking the entrance and a red Audi next to the house. "They're here."

"Good. They don't know I sent everyone across the road to Dimpsey's place."

"So, how do you wanna do this?"

"JC has Trevor, so we can't just storm the place. We'll have to—"

Case stopped talking when he felt his phone buzzing. He

pulled the phone from the pocket of his suit coat and looked at the screen—Sam.

"Sam, are you okay?"

Sam's voice came across in a rush, "Case, they're here."

"What do you mean? We just spotted them at the farm. You're at Dimpsey's place, right?"

"No, Case. I'm in our house—with Prissy. She called to warn me when she escaped from the motel. I had her meet me here, just in case it was a trap. Then JC and the other guy showed up before we could leave."

Case felt his heart hammering in his chest, "Okay. Where are you right now?"

"We're in the bedroom. I watched them split up. I think they're circling around the property and moving toward the back of the house. JC has Trevor."

Case pulled to the side of the road and threw the big Yukon into park. "Listen to me, Sam. You and Prissy need to fend them off until Mike and I can get to the house. Where's your pistol?"

"I've got it with me."

"Okay. I need you to cover the back of the house from the bedroom windows. Don't pull the trigger unless you have a clear shot. JC's not going to expose himself, so he'll use Trevor as cover. Mike and I will draw their attention to the front of the house and come up that way. If they get inside, hide. Can you do that for me?"

Sam thought about everything Case had done for her and Mia—the risks he'd taken to save them both. In situations like this, there wasn't a man in the world that she trusted more. "Okay. I can do that. I love you, Case."

Sam was brave, but Case could hear the fear in her voice. "I love you too, Sam."

Case hung up the phone as Mike stood outside the door, looking toward the house.

"JC has the kid. He's moving around the back. I can't see Vince." Mike reported.

Case threw the big armored Yukon into drive. "There'll be some vests and a couple of HK 416s in the back. Grab those, get in, and buckle up."

Chapter 41

JC and Vince were rounding opposite corners of the back porch when they heard the sound of crashing metal and breaking glass. JC looked back toward the road to see the mangled Suburban pushed to the edge of the driveway and the big armored Yukon barreling toward the house in a cloud of dust.

"Go now!" JC said, pointing toward the backdoor.

Vince did as he was told and rushed inside with his AR up and at the ready, but JC didn't follow. Instead, he pushed Trevor toward the barn.

"Get moving, kid," JC said as he grabbed Trevor by the collar and forced him forward. He needed to make it to the barn before Case realized he wasn't in the house. He wanted to kill the kid just to make a point but knew he needed him if he expected to make it out of this godforsaken town alive. He shoved Trevor again just because it made him feel better.

"If you just let me go and turn yourself in, you'll be okay. Case doesn't want to hurt people anymore, but he will if you make him."

JC kept pushing Trevor forward, "Did I fucking ask you?"

Gravel flew from beneath the big Pirelli run-flat tires of the Yukon as Case slid into the driveway next to the house. Whoever was inside opened fire. Glass shattered from the left side windows of the living room as rounds pelted the black-painted metal of the hood, quickly working their way up to the ballistic windshield, like lethal drops of rain. Case and Mike had each been in situations like this before. They knew the UL-7-rated glass could take multiple high-caliber rounds in the same spot before shattering. Both men sat calmly as the rounds impacted inches from their face, checking the chambers of their 416s, waiting for their opportunity to attack. It didn't take long. Whoever was firing from the house emptied their thirty rounds and had paused to reload. That gave them the precious seconds they needed to act.

"Move!"

"Moving!" Mike responded as both men bailed out of the Yukon and sprinted toward the nearest cover.

Case took refuge behind one of the big red maples next to the house, but once the shooter was back up and firing, Mike got pinned down behind the Yukon. He signaled for Case to lay down suppressive fire. As Case opened up on the living room window, Mike sprinted to the back of the house and took cover behind a large pile of firewood, then provided cover for Case as he sprinted to the opposite corner of the house outside the shooter's field of view.

With both men safe from the opposition, they kept their muzzles up and pointed at the house while making their way to the back.

Wood splintered above Case's head, and he instinctively dove behind the concrete blocks that supported the porch.

"Get in the house, Mike! That has to be JC firing from the barn. I'll cover you, then move to him. He has Trevor."

Mike nodded and sprinted toward the back door. Case didn't want to risk hitting Trevor, so he sent a barrage of bullets over the barn to keep JC's head down as he raced toward the ancient white oak that sat between him and the barn. Once safely behind cover, Case quickly swapped magazines to ensure his weapon was topped off, and checked the expended mag for rounds. There were a few left, so he stuck the magazine in his back pocket and peeked around the tree.

Case could see movement from the hay loft. He'd need to swing wide around the barn and come in from the back if he expected to get the drop on JC, but with Mike inside the house, that would leave him open and exposed. There was no way to manage the confrontation without putting himself or Trevor in danger. If JC were as big a coward as Mike suggested, he'd use Trevor as cover to get clear of the barn. The only thing Case could do now was stall or offer to turn himself over to JC in exchange for the boy. He needed time until Mike was out of the house and could back him up. The best way to do that was to get JC talking.

"I know who you are and why you're hear JC. You're here because I killed your friends in Richmond."

JC laughed. "You think that's why I'm here? I could give a fuck less about those dirty assholes."

"Then tell me why? Why are you doing this?"

"Because you're an impediment, Case, and I need you gone."

"I know what it is you want JC. You think I'm supposed to let you and your boys, do whatever you want here in Pikesville? Running drugs and feeding these girls to Tanner. It's not happening as long as I'm alive."

"Well, you're not gonna be alive much longer now are you, Case. So, you can either shut the fuck up and stop stalling, or I'll kill the kid right now and let you watch."

Case looked back toward the house. Still no sign of Mike. "There's no need for the boy to get hurt. Just tell me what you need me to do."

"Toss the fucking rifle, now, and step out so I can see you."

Case was out of options. With Mike still out of the picture, he had no support. JC had the upper hand and Case knew it, so he reluctantly tossed the AR into the field, hoping that JC wouldn't suspect the Glock 19 he had tucked into his waistband.

Prissy and Sam peeked through the slats of the bi-fold closet doors. Sam gripped her Sig P365 MACRO tightly while Prissy held shakily onto the Glock she'd stolen from Vince. They looked worriedly at each other when they heard the old wooden floor creak just outside the door. Vince slowly stepped around the corner with his rifle shouldered and swept the room. Prissy panicked and pulled the trigger.

Vince stumbled backward just as Mike appeared from the far side of the hallway. Both men saw each other and fired at once. Mike's bullet struck Vince in the center of his head, dropping him immediately, but the second went wide, missing its target completely. Mike fought to find balance, confused by his body's inability to cooperate. He reached down with his support hand to check himself for injuries and came up with a blood-soaked hand.

Prissy saw Vince down in the hallway and rushed from the closet to find Mike slumped against the wall, bleeding from his abdomen.

She ran to the man's side with big tears forming in the corners her eyes, "Jesus, Mike. Are you okay?"

Mike tried to compose himself. He knew he was dying but didn't want Prissy's last image of him to be one of weakness. He'd given into weakness one too many times in his life, so today, he would die with dignity.

"Don't be scared Priscilla. It's gonna be okay."

Prissy sobbed as Sam ran from the bedroom and knelt beside her. "Sam, we have to do something. We have to help Mike. He's not a bad man like JC and the others."

Sam could see Mike was fading fast, so she wrapped her arms around the girl and held on tight. "Prissy, It's too late. I'm so sorry."

"No!" Prissy screamed as Mike gripped her tiny hand.

The blood filling his abdomen put pressure on his lungs, making it hard for him to speak.

"Listen, kid," Mike said between strangled breaths. "You've got a life ahead of you now. Case is gonna get JC and you'll be free of all of this." Mike looked down at the blood soaking his shirt and pooling on the floor around him, "I want you to do me a favor though, okay?"

"Anything, Mike."

"I want you to start over, Prissy. Your past doesn't dictate who you are. You can have a life here. These are good people. I want you to stay. I just wish I could stay with you."

Prissy looked up at Sam, who nodded quietly.

"Okay, Mike. I promise."

Mike smiled and gripped Prissy's hand tightly. His breathing became raspy and shallow. Prissy felt his grip slacken, as his hand slipped to the floor. He was gone.

Prissy wept as Sam held the grieving girl tight. "It's okay, Prissy. It's okay."

Chapter 42

Dimpsey heard the distinct sound of rifle fire coming from across the road. Trevor was in danger, and he couldn't sit still any longer. Hate filled the man's heart as he grabbed the old 30-30 from Mia's hands and strode toward the door.

"Amanda, you stay here with Mia till I get back."

"Dimpsey, Is that a good idea?"

The old man turned to Amanda before walking out and shook his head, "Probably not, but that's my grandson over there and the only family I have left. I'll be damned if I'm gonna just sit here and let him get hurt."

Amanda could see the determination in the man's eyes and nodded. He was a warrior and there'd be no stopping him. "Go. I'll hold this down while you're gone. But please be careful, Dimpsey."

Case pressed himself against the trunk of the old oak and closed his eyes, "You have me dead to rights, JC. But I'm not moving until you agree to let the boy go. You do that, and you and I can settle this like men."

JC wasn't stupid. He knew he needed Trevor to get out of this alive.

"No way, Case. But here's what I'll do. I'll walk out with the boy, and you'll step out from behind that tree. I'll let him go and wait for him to reach the house before I shoot you dead—how's that sound?"

Case contemplated his odds. He knew JC would kill him as soon as he broke cover and probably shoot Trevor as well, so he press-checked the Glock he had stashed behind his belt and covered it with the tail of his shirt to keep it hidden from JC's view. It was about sixty yards from his position to the barn door—a difficult shot with a pistol but doable. The trick would be getting his rounds off first once Trevor was outside the line of fire. JC wouldn't be so careful, so Case knew he needed to move fast.

"Okay, JC. We'll do it your way. But I need to see you walk out with Trevor first."

There was a period of silence before Case heard the squeal of rusty hinges and watched as the large barn door swung open slowly.

"Here he is, Case." JC said, shoving Trevor toward the barn door and pointing the gun at him." You have five seconds to step out from behind that tree, or I shoot the boy instead, and we'll see how this plays out."

Case took a deep breath and stepped out from behind the tree with his hands at shoulder level.

JC wanted to live and knew this was his last chance. If he could get clear of Case and make it to New York, he'd be safe under the protection of Tanner Greene, but right now, everyone in Pikesville wanted him dead. Case was likely still armed, and JC knew he'd fight to the death to protect Sam and the boy. His only option now was to leverage the information he had on Trevor's mother to affect an escape. JC gripped the kid tight and bent close to Trevor's ear.

"Listen to me closely, kid. I know your mom—Tina

Campbell, right?"

Trevor felt the breath catch in his throat. His mom had been in a bad way after his dad died. Over the years, he'd given up hope of ever seeing her again, so to hear someone speak her name after all this time tore at the boy's emotions.

"You know where she's at? Is she okay?" Trevor asked.

"I know exactly where she's at kid, but if you ever want to see her again, you'd better make damned sure your friend out there doesn't kill me. I'm the only person who knows how to find her, so when I let you go, you're going to run straight toward Case out there and tell him not to shoot. You understand? You stay directly between me and him. Now, run, boy!" JC said, kicking at Trevor, who sprinted toward Case, screaming.

"Case! Don't shoot! Please!" But no one heard.

Case made his move. Both hands dropped to his waistline. His left hand grasped his shirt, raising it to expose the grip of his Glock 19, while his right hand brought the weapon into the center of his body, but he didn't go any further than that. Trevor was running straight toward him, staying in the line of fire. He couldn't risk taking the shot.

Everything seemed to move in slow motion as JC raised the rifle. But before he could get the gun up to his shoulder, someone fired. Case knew it wasn't him, and he didn't see JC get a round off. He watched as Trevor stopped cold in his tracks. Shock and terror spread across the boy's face as he turned slowly back toward the barn. JC dropped the rifle and fell to his knees as a look of confusion spread across his face. That's when Case saw the blood pouring from JC's chest and Dimpsey stepping from the edge of the back porch—the Henry rifle pressed firmly into his shoulder. He'd waited there, out of sight, until Trevor was clear of JC. The old man worked the lever and shot one final time, dropping JC to the ground.

Trevor stood, locked in place, staring at the lifeless body of the man who'd held him captive. He turned toward Case and saw that he was still standing. He was elated to see that Case was okay but devastated by the realization that the only chance he had of finding his mom was now lying dead in a field.

"You okay, Case?" Dimpsey asked without taking his eyes off JC's body.

"I'm good Dimpsey. You showed up just in time."

"We'll settle up later. Where's Sam?"

Just as Case was about to speak, Sam came running through the backdoor with Prissy in tow.

"Case!"

Case ran to meet Sam and noticed that Prissy's hands were covered in blood.

"What happened to Mike?" Case asked.

"He's gone." Prissy said, hanging her head.

Case didn't need an explanation. He knew Mike went out the way he wanted to—fighting for something worthwhile.

"What do we do now?" Sam asked.

Case looked down at JC's body. It was still, almost peaceful. Blood seeped slowly from the fatal wounds into the dirt outside the barn. But this wasn't over. Trevor watched quietly, not saying a word.

"We call Bobby and Dillon. They'll have some backup at Maple Grove by now. We need to get the police out here as soon as we can. But first, I need to make a phone call."

Case knelt and searched JC's body until he found what he was looking for—a cell phone. He grabbed the dead man by the hair and raised his face to the screen, using the facial recognition software to unlock it. Once opened, Case dropped JC's face back into the bloody dirt and stepped away. Prissy cringed at the coldness of it all.

Case scrolled through the recent calls and found the number to Tanner Greene, then hit dial. After a few rings, a soft, nasally voice answered.

"It's about time. Is it done?"

Case's face turned hard as stone. This is the man who was pulling the strings. The real reason everything went so bad in Pikesville. "No, it isn't Tanner. Not yet, anyway."

There was a brief silence before Tanner spoke again. "Younger?"

"You're goddamned right it's me. Your men failed you, Tanner. Now I'm going to find you, and when I do, I'm going to make you regret the day you ever heard that name."

Case hung the phone up and stuck it in his pocket. There was a lot more information on it he'd need for what he was about to do.

Chapter 43

It had been a long evening. The late-day sun finally dipped below the western ridge, casting its final light across the farm. Prissy stood there watching stoically as paramedics loaded Mike's body into the ambulance. She'd been around men her entire life, some bad, some worse, but Mike had been different. He'd never been very talkative, but she could tell by how he acted that he genuinely cared about her. It was a new feeling and one that she would miss.

Bobby and Amanda stood with Detective Wayne, Case, and Dimpsey as CSI personnel took pictures of JC's lifeless body, laying in the blood-soaked soil by the barn. From the outside, the scene must have seemed surreal with everyone dressed for a wedding, yet surrounded by the aftermath of extreme violence. Trevor stood in the yard talking quietly to Mia, who looked as if she were about to cry. From Prissy's perspective, it appeared that everything was finally over, but Sam knew better.

"You doin' all right?" Sam asked, placing her hand on Prissy's shoulder.

Prissy nodded. "I'm just glad to see it over."

Sam didn't know what to say. "Prissy, this isn't over yet, sweetheart."

"What do you mean?"

"Did you know about Tanner Greene?"

"The man Case just called? I've heard JC talking to him on the phone. I don't know who he is, but he seemed to be the man everyone answers to."

"He is, and he's still out there, Prissy. He and other men like him are responsible for everything that's happened to you and those other girls. He's a monster."

"And now Case is going to go after him?" Prissy asked.

"Yes, he will, but he won't do it alone."

Just then, Sam saw the old Dodge truck that once belonged to Case's dad coming up the driveway. Ross stepped out of the passenger side wearing a shirt that was one size too small. There was a picture of a teddy bear holding balloons on the front. The words *Get Well Soon* arched across the top—an obvious purchase from the hospital gift shop. Matt walked from the driver's side, still dressed in his blue suit.

"Sorry we missed all the action," Matt said.

Sam smiled. "You need to talk to Case. I think there's still plenty of action to be had if that's what you're looking for."

Ross walked past Prissy on his way to the barn, "Action is my middle name, ma'am." He said, winking. Prissy and Sam both smiled. Despite the seriousness of the situation, Ross always had a way of lightening the mood.

As the two men joined the others by the barn, Sam turned back to Prissy. "Were you serious when you told Mike you would stay here?"

"I have nowhere to go, Sam. I don't know what to do."

Since meeting Prissy in the bar, Sam had thought long and hard about the girl's situation. "I think what's most important right now is to keep you clean and sober. If you'd like, I have a place I'm putting up for rent in town. You're more than welcome to stay there for a while. As far as work goes, I could use some help at the bar while Crystal recovers. I can waive the first few months' rent until we get you settled and on your feet."

Prissy looked at Sam without speaking. The unfamiliar shock of receiving human kindness evident on her face.

"You don't have to decide anything right now. We have a spare room here until you figure out what you want to do."

With no words to express her gratitude, Prissy wrapped her arms around Sam and squeezed. Nothing she could ever say would repay the kindness these people had shown her. She could only clean herself up and let her actions do the talking for her. She looked over at the barn as JC's body was zipped into a large black bag and loaded into another ambulance. This was the freedom she had always dreamed of, and she wasn't about to let it pass her by.

Bobby and Dillon Wayne stood with Case, finishing their notes as Matt and Ross rounded the corner. Case excused himself and met his former coworkers before they made it to the barn.

"So, what's the prognosis?" Case asked, nodding his head toward Ross.

"It's just a flesh wound. No big deal."

"Yeah, a thirty-five-stitch flesh wound," Matt added.

"Will you be good enough to help me finish this up?"

"What do you mean?" Matt asked, "There's more to this?"

"JC was just a flunky looking to move up the ladder. Tanner Greene's the man behind it all. He's the one responsible for the operation that was running through Cook County. JC and the Dead Rebels were his conduit into New York. That's all been destroyed now, but if Tanner's not dealt with, everything we've done up to this point was for nothing. He'll either come after me again or just find another route through someplace just like

Pikesville, and more girls will get hurt."

Matt stood quietly while Ross typed something into his phone.

"Got him." Ross said, "Tanner Greene, CEO of Stonehill Investment Group." Ross tapped on the tiny screen again, "He also sits on the board for multiple Fortune 500 companies and has ties to politics—world leaders. This guy's definitely the head of the snake."

"So, what do you want to do?" Matt asked.

Case looked back at the house. Sam stood beside Prissy, consoling the girl. Mia sat on the back porch steps, holding Trevor's hands, trying to bring the boy down from the adrenaline rush he'd just experienced. Less than a year ago, she'd suffered the same fate, so she knew what he was feeling. Case couldn't let that happen again—not to the people he loved—not ever. He knew what needed to be done.

"If Tanner Greene's the head of the snake, then we go to New York, and we cut it off."

"We?" Matt asked. "You coming back to the team?"

Case looked out over the farm as night settled in. "Dimpsey, you got things under control here until I can get back?"

Dimpsey nodded, "You know I do, Case."

"Alright then. Let's get Andre on the phone and get this ball rolling. We have work to do."

Epilogue

Tanner Greene sat alone in his office, staring blankly at the phone. He'd waited patiently for the call from JC telling him that Case Younger was dead, but that's not how things turned out. If Younger had JC's phone it was safe to assume JC and the others were dead, and if everything he knew about Case was true, he'd need to get out of the city as soon as possible. He'd also need to make sure Case couldn't follow him. Tanner shoved the phone into his pocket and hit the button on his desk. Celia's voice came over the speaker immediately.

"Yes, Mr. Greene."

"Celia, get Senator Whitlock on the phone. Tell him something's broken in New York, and I'm going to need fixers. He'll know what that means."

"Yes, sir. Right away."

Tanner stood by the windows behind his desk, looking over the city. He thought about everything he'd built and how one man now stood to destroy it all. Greene wasn't about to stand by and let that happen. Senator Whitlock owed him and had the resources to stop Case before he reached the city, but that wouldn't be enough. With three of his top men out of the picture, he'd need to lay low for a while. Tanner walked back to the desk and called again for Celia.

"Yes, sir."

"Celia, pack your bags. I think it's time you and I left the city for a while."

Celia was smart enough to know if Tanner was leaving the

city, something had gone terribly wrong. Her mind turned to Mike, the only man in this god-awful place who had ever shown her any kindness. She doubted she would ever see him again.

"Yes, sir. I'll be ready to go immediately."

When the line went dead, Tanner sat at his desk. A war was coming, and it was a war he had no intention of fighting himself—the stakes were too high. If his cards were played correctly, he could hide at his estate in the Catskills until Whitlock cleaned this mess up, then business could continue as usual. But only after Case Younger was gone forever.

Acknowledgements

I'd like to thank my wife and kids for being my first readers and the sounding board for all my big ideas (even the bad ones). These stories wouldn't exist without you. Thank you to the outstanding team at YMAA Publication Center and especially to my brilliant editor, Leslie Takao, whose patient guidance has molded this series into something I couldn't have managed alone. Thanks also to my friends, subject matter experts, and fellow writers, Delbert Roll, Jeff Clark, Alan Mack, and Liz Lazarus, for their input and guidance. To Cynthia Taylor and Pages Books and Coffee in Mount Airy, North Carolina (www.pagesbooksandcoffee.com), for being the launch site for *Homecoming* and the Case Younger Series. I look forward to working with you again in the future. I'd also like to thank all the incredible folks at the International Thriller Writers organization. The level of support and guidance I've received from everyone I've encountered there has been truly remarkable. Keep up the fantastic work. Finally, I'd like to extend my warmest appreciation to my friend and fellow movie buff, Jude Gerard Prest, writer, director, producer, and CEO of LifeLike Productions, who sees potential in Case Younger beyond the written page.

About the Author

GARY QUESENBERRY Gary Quesenberry is an Army veteran and career Federal Air Marshal with an extensive background in both domestic and foreign counter-terror operations. Gary retired from federal service in 2020 and returned to his hometown of Hillsville, Virginia, in the Blue Ridge Mountains. He is the award-winning author of four nonfiction books on the topics of situational awareness and personal safety: *Spotting Danger Before It Spots You, Spotting Danger Before It Spots Your Kids, Spotting Danger Before It Spots Your Teens,* and *Spotting Danger for Travelers.* Visit him at GaryQuesenberry.com and follow along on Instagram at @gary.quesenberry.

www.ingramcontent.com/pod-product-compliance
Lightning Source LLC
Jackson TN
JSHW081219170725
87770JS00002B/56